To Liz with
for your

The End

ALAN PLATT

www.theendtheendtheend.com

The End

Typeset in Garamond Pro and Futura Medium.

Published by Final

ISBN 978-616-593-741-2

www.theendtheendtheend.com

The Pentagraph

Cajun moon, where does your power lie,
As you move across the Southern sky?
You took my baby away too soon.
What have you done, Cajun moon?

JJ Cale

'I just wanna know who did who,
and who got the two bucks.'

Madame Joy

The End

This is the story of a rock god. Literally.

It will be the only true telling of the global phenomenon that was Omega Finn, the rock star known by his followers as The End, a young man who became a religion.

It was authorized by Omega Finn himself. I was there from the beginning of the cult to its spectacular and horrific unraveling.

Put simply, this is the tragedy of a boy who pretended to have magical powers. And of a girl who really did.

Alan Platt

One

In retrospect, it seems inevitable that someone like him would emerge onto the world stage and dominate it so completely. But before it happened, nobody ever imagined an Omega Finn.

Looking back, it all seems so meticulously planned, the rise and rise of a young Southern charmer of reasonably good looks and talent, to heights undreamed of. By anyone. Ever.

But there was no plan. No dream. Not even much ambition to speak of, at the beginning.

Even the young man himself could not have imagined the phenomenon that he became, and which he pushed so far, so fast.

It all began with one tiny stroke of destiny. And even that didn't seem anything special at the time. It was just a weird occurrence that might have had no significance at all. But it changed the world. Well, a good slice of the world, anyway. For a while.

It happened on a plane. A young singer in a band that few had heard of outside of Louisiana and New Orleans, was flying Economy Class from somewhere to somewhere else, chatting amiably with a stranger in the next seat, to pass the time. The guy was an oldish man, a professor of geology, his name unimportant. The young singer's name was Oliver Finnegan.

But young Oliver was fascinated with the things the old guy was telling him and sat in rapt attention, surprising himself by being so taken with a subject he had previously had very little interest in. Earthquakes.

The old geologist was a world authority on them. And he was one of those natural teachers, so excited by their subject that their enthusiasm is infectious. But he had Oliver's complete attention for another reason, too. He believed he had proof that very soon a very destructive quake was about to hit a totally unexpected place.

New York City.

Oliver had friends in New York, and knew the city a little. So even if this earthquake dude was full of crap with his crazy ideas, the mere thought of those canyons of Manhattan with their giant towers quivering and cracking and, God forbid, even falling, had him hanging on the guy's every word. And the picture he painted was vivid, horrifying, truly catastrophic. He knew how to lay it on in full color, the probable loss of life, the shaking and crumbling of the most magnificent of cities.

Even if the quake were a small one, which he said it probably would be, the result would be devastating, at a huge cost in life and property, because no one was prepared. Apparently it was widely known that there is a fault line under New York. But it had always been dismissed as dormant, and basically forgotten. But this guy was on his way to a big geology conference to present scary new findings. He had detected movement, tiny but significant, using some new hypersensitive device. And he was of sufficient standing in the field that he would be taken seriously and his warning might alert New York City to assess response times and so on, just in case. This was a very big deal and Oliver totally got it.

So he offered his help to re-arrange the files and graphs in the guy's laptop, and was given the password. They sat side by side, the laptop on Oliver's knee, going through it all until he had the old man's presentation well organized and down cold.

Then the weird thing that changed the world happened. The old man died. Just. Like. That.

Professor Whatsisname just keeled right over and face-planted into the seat in front with such a smack that the guy in front got up and turned around and yelled at him, "Hey, what the fuck are you doing, man?!"

He was dying, that's what. In fact he was dead before he hit the back of the seat in front of him.

Heart attack, stroke, whatever, Oliver never knew nor asked. He was so completely shaken by this horrific event - a guy he was just getting to know and like and respect, dying right next to him - that he could barely function for the next hour or so, as the plea went out over the PA for a doctor, then the realization that this dude was way past needing one, then the awful decision to simply leave him where he was, dead, in the seat next to Oliver, with a blanket placed over him, and the ghoulish rubbernecking of the passengers, a few of whom even snapped shots for social media, as Oliver, close to tears and totally freaked, turned his face into the window and kept it there until they landed and hauled the poor dead bastard out of his seat and rushed Oliver off the plane and through some perfunctory questions as to what he knew, which was nothing, and he found himself in a taxi headed for wherever it was he was going, where he sleepwalked into a bar and knocked back many shots of Jack Daniels to stop himself shaking and only then realized, as he opened his backpack, that the cabin crew had stuffed the dead guy's laptop in there in all the confusion, assuming it was his because it was on his knee.

Half hammered with bourbon, and still half catatonic, he slowly and woozily came to the mind-boggling conclusion that he, Oliver Finnegan, rock 'n' roll nobody, a teenager from the backwater bayous of Louisiana, deep in the heart of picturesque Cajun country, father unknown, mother deceased, claimed as family only by an old Cajun grandma, may be the sole owner of something literally earth-shaking, a piece of knowledge that could turn out to be absolute, total, freaking dynamite.

Two

Deep in the jungle. Deep in Amazonia. Deep in deepest Brazil. A deep so deep there are no names, no maps, no nothing. A jungle so thick that there are tribes a few miles apart that have never met.

This is where they found her. She was - as close as they could guess - around fourteen or so, maybe less. If they had tried to find her they never could have, nor her village nor her tribe. There are tribes in there so lost, they never will be found nor do they want to be. They're fine just how and where they are, thank you, and have been so for a thousand years or so, give or take.

She was found by a fluke. A fluke of rain. A fluke of nature. A fluke of flood, the Rio Negro flood. Every year the spider web of a thousand little tributaries of the big Rio Negro gets flooded so fast that it's engulfed in seconds, like a big sudden wave bearing down through the trees, a wave so big you could surf it, and it picks up everything in its path that is not rooted in the ground. Twigs, branches, monkeys, pigs, people fishing and young girls singing without a care in the world while they bathe on the riverbank.

Whoosh. It's on you and you're up and gone, and maybe you can grab onto something and find your way home or maybe you bang your head and you drown and your corpse is swept out into a bigger stream and then a bigger and bigger one, until it joins the massive roaring river swollen brown and crazy with the rains and it floats you out into the deep, deep roiling water and you get eaten by the piranha, and the bones they leave sink to the bottom and show up in polished little bits on a riverbank far, far away and get carved into something cute years later, and worn around someone's neck and that's you, baby. Hi, there. You're jewelry.

She got found on a log, floating half conscious, god knows how many, many miles from where she was swept up, she and a little green lizard of a species nobody had seen before.

The old guy who spotted her was one of those crazy Europeans who just can't get far enough away from whatever they didn't like about home, and he had been gone so long he was nut brown and naked, but would reluctantly admit to having once been English.

He lived on fishing and foraging and had a pretty fine little treehouse up high above the floodline, slung among gigantic fig trees in the company of monkeys who stole his catch and helped him shoo off the snakes.

Up there is where he carried her, a naked girl slung over his naked old shoulder, and up there is where she came around and got fussed over and poked and prodded by local village women who could not understand a word she said, so they called her Macumba.

Macumba is the religion of the jungle. Macumba is magic. Good magic. Black magic. Believers think that some folks simply embody Macumba. They *are* Macumba. And, looking at this pretty little vision who was jabbering some gibberish they had never heard before, with a bone through her bottom lip pointing down at her chin and her little pet green lizard, she might just as well have been Macumba incarnate. Voodoo. She had it. They knew it.

The former Englishman, who up until then had been tolerated by the locals on the river, then accepted reluctantly as one might accept a slightly nutty old uncle, became suddenly fawned over and revered. It was to him, after all, that the magical girl had appeared. To him it was that the little voodoo goddess had first materialized, impossibly, mysteriously, on that holy day. And it was he who had carried her up into her altar in the trees above the bend of the big, brown, roaring river, where the monkeys brought her things they had never brought to him - new strange fruits and shiny shells and bright blue bugs with golden wings.

Three

Oliver's little posse of teenage boys had grown up in those picturesque Louisiana swamps known as the bayous, west of New Orleans, in what they call Cajun country, in a remote little parish known as Mama Boo, postcard cute, moss hanging from the boughs of the big old trees, reflected in the water. Like most of Cajun country, it was pretty much all water, shallow and muddy, full of catfish and gators. Food and fear.

All water. Nowhere to dig. So in the bayous there are no graveyards. Instead, the dead rest above ground in tiny tombs, like toy villages of little stone houses. Much more pleasant for them. And spooky.

Spooky is word you hear a lot around Cajun country, voodoo country, with its spells and potions, magic charms, midnite rites and witchy women.

All water. And big trees. Like a drowned forest. Pretty as can be in the evening around sunset, when it's pure magic. But you get lost in here, boy, and you're good and lost. Step into the wrong stretch of water, and the aligators will put you in a cute little stone house.

As with many another kid down here, nobody was quite sure who little Ollie's papa was, but it was academic since he'd only been passing through and was long gone. His mother was dead, a pretty woman, they say, working at whatever she could find, and while sitting out on a verandah with a few friends one evening, having fun, minding her business, she caught a bullet meant for somebody else, and nobody ever found out who that somebody else might be, or who had fired the gun, or even what direction the shot had come from, an open and shut case of what the fuck.

But he was never alone. This was a tight community with their sweet dialect, accordion music and easy attitude, so he grew up surrounded by affection and other Cajun kids his own age, and he held one trump card. A grandma who loved him to bits. And this was not just any old grandma. This was Madame Joy.

Madame Joy was a legend, tough as nails and sweeter than honey from the bee, except for when the bee was in her bonnet. Which was much of the time. She had a boatload of opinions, all of them vocal and to express them, a tongue that could strip paint.

You knew where you stood with Madame Joy.

It was she who organized four bad boys into a band to keep them out of the kind of trouble they had a tendency to be in.

Trouble around here was not usually with the police. Those guys sensibly stayed away from Mama Boo. It was with neighbors. And if one of them came after you, you would wish you were merely in trouble with the cops. Hotwire a car or two and you might be in jail for a night or two. But fool with some guy's daughter around here and the gators might be snacking on a finger or two.

So Madame 'acquired' a bunch of guitars and amps - no questions asked - and set the boys to learning how to make a few bucks out of them. She would sit there on the back porch with a catfish line in the water and plugs in her ears and suffer along with the 'musicians' as they strangulated a few chords and murdered a few simple songs on the road to not sounding too horrible and setting the hounds howling.

The house, on stilts among the big trees and the hanging moss, was a local landmark. 'Madame Joy' was emblazoned in gaudy script in yellows, greens and reds with stars and planets, a bit faded now since the days when it was on the side of a real gypsy caravan pulled by a horse, part of the traveling carnival that had plied the small towns of the Deep South and that she had been a part of in those old days when 'carney' people were local stars, never still, pitching tents and barely staying ahead of the law. And she still kept up her sideline, reading tarot cards and palms for the locals for miles around, who swore by her 'gift', mostly just gifted bullshit, reading the customer more than their cards or their palms, saying what they wanted to hear, but occasionally surprising Madame herself with an insight or a timely warning, so that over the years, she had begun to doubt her own doubts about it all, and to wonder if maybe there really was something behind it all and if maybe she really did have a connection with another reality outside the reality we think of as reality.

Mostly, such thoughts did not trouble her sleep. She was just making a buck plying her trade in honest speculation, no harm done, cheering folks up and being paid as much for her wonderful company and shrewd advice over a cup of tea or a shot of hooch, as for her star charts and fairy tales. And she was not above occasionally getting her hooks into some rich sucker from Lafayette or Baton Rouge who wanted to get in touch with a dead husband or a dead cat currently floating around in limbo on 'the other side'.

When the dogs quit howling, Madame Joy figured the boys were near enough ready to audition, which they did at a local roadhouse and, of course, got the gig. You did not say no to Madame.

They were allowed to play only after lunch and before dinner, when the staff were the only music critics and no actual paying customers might feel a sudden inclination to eat elsewhere.

But pretty soon they were really not too bad, and after a month or so, they were allowed to play for the paying public, Mondays only, when they could not do too much damage to the reputation of the joint, and with a local fiddler added to the line-up, a wrinkly old boy, a virtuoso who picked up the slack and basically played every note that mattered.

Cajun two-steps and much-requested line dances led to a bit of slightly cooler rock 'n' roll from time to time, and because they were so young and cute, and after they ditched the old fiddler, they got a following among the local girls, with Moms keeping an eye on them and Dads packing heat. And it wasn't too long before they were booking gigs farther afield, at first not so far away that Madame Joy, their manager, was not known and feared, but then more and more distant from her protective radius, getting booked on pure merit as a pretty cool rock band, with that Southern swampy New Orleans sound, funky, sexy and danceable.

They didn't have a band name. Bar owners just referred to them as the place they were from. So when they finally did cut loose and go out on the road all over Louisiana and Alabama and Mississippi, like a real rock outfit, that's the name that stuck. Mama Boo.

Four

If you're looking for a city that's truly, hopelessly, off the beaten track, try Manaus.

Stick a pin in the dead center of the Amazonian rainforest and there it is, in all its gory glory.

Outside of its built-up area with its few tall buildings and big roads, there are square miles of dwellings so wretched that only in their wildest dreams would they aspire to being called slums.

Rivers in this part of the world are so wide they might as well be oceans to the folks living there. Manaus is stuck between the two biggest of them all, the Amazon and the Rio Negro, rivers so wide there is no 'other side', even with binoculars, and so dangerous you don't even think about it.

So there it sits, thousands of miles from anywhere, hemmed in between two raging torrents, both miles wide, and encircled by a jungle the size of a planet.

Manaus is so remote, so lost, so far away from anywhere else, that it might as well not be there at all, for all the world cares.

This is where the old village women brought little Macumba, jabbering away to her lizard in her own sing-song language and in the few words of English the old man had taught her.

Even with the white bone through her lower lip, she was still the prettiest girl anyone had ever seen, with eyes the color of gold and pale gold skin and frizzy golden hair to match.

This was a few months after she had been saved by the old man, and they were still trying to put clothes on her nakedness, and she was still throwing them off with curses, apart from which she rarely spoke, except to the little lizard that she called Teetoo. So the old girls let her walk around naked and made sure she didn't wander into the street and meet a local pimp who would not believe his luck.

They were staying with a woman who was once connected with their village. And they carried a letter of introduction from the old Englishman to a another old man they were very anxious to meet.

He was an ethnologist, an ethnographer, an anthropologist, an ethno-philologist and an anthropo-linguist - in other words, a guy who might understand one word Macumba said. Nobody else did. This man was the real thing. He'd been everywhere it was possible to go in that rainforest and then some. He'd met every remote tribe anybody had ever heard of and recorded some of the weirdest languages known to man and a few unknown to man. The old English guy on the river had taken care of him once, years before, on one of his trips, which is how the women had his address. Best of all was the fact that he was a very sweet old fellow, a college professor, a kind, caring, softly-spoken, gentle, white-haired old Swede named Olaf.

They had covered Macumba in a wrap of some sort to keep her respectable in public transport on their way to his office on a local college campus. She had been her usual sullen, non-communicative self up to that point. But when she was ushered into his office and saw the old professor at his desk, everything changed.

Was it the white hair? Was it that he reminded her of the other old man who had saved her and fed her and been so kind to her?

Whatever the reason, she immediately pulled herself away from the women, yanked off her wrap and threw it on the floor, walked up to the distinguished old gent totally naked, stood before him for a moment, and then, to everybody's astonishment, sat down on his knee, jabbering away to him like they were old friends and handed him her little lizard to hold.

The professor never missed a beat. He just smiled sweetly as if this was the most normal thing, paid complete attention to her strange prattle and managed, miraculously, to grasp the meaning of some of it.

Slowly, bit by bit, with her getting occasionally impatient at his very limited understanding, they established a few basic principles and with him being the great linguist that he was, they got into a groove and started to really talk to each other. He even managed to ask her a few questions, and she answered them.

He found out many things about her. Her real name, for a start. It was something that involved strange clicks, and she laughed out loud when he hopelessly tried to pronounce it. It was the first time she had laughed since she showed up on the log, and the women were shocked by her sweet girly giggle. So, since he couldn't say her real name, he just addressed her as Macumba and she seemed not to mind.

Then he did something unexpected and brilliant. He slid her off his knee and, taking her by the hand - she let him - he walked her out of the study, asking the women to stay put, and took her into his private quarters adjacent. There he opened a wardrobe and showed her a rack of girl's clothing that his granddaughter, about Macumba's age, kept in Manaus for her occasional visits - a few thin cotton frocks, shorts and blouses that were too flimsy for Swedish weather. He indicated that she could try them on, and stood back and watched her as, for the first time, she was confronted with so many colorful things and allowed to choose.

She went straight for a cheap plastic tiara and put it on her head while Olaf, who may have been sorely tempted to take a photo of such a beautiful girl standing there wearing only a crown, sat back and lit a pipe. She stood naked in front of the rack of clothes for several minutes, scratching her butt and looking at them all in a very solemn way. This would, after all, be a very solemn moment for any teenage girl.

With Olaf's gentle help, she learned how to work a button and a zipper and a clasp and a velcro fastener, and bit by bit, becoming more and more at ease with posing in front of the wardrobe's full-length mirror, admiring herself and asking Olaf's opinion - he applauded everything - she made her choice.

Everything. She chose everything. Every teeshirt, skirt, blouse, sandal and high heel shoe, plus one truly show-stopping article, a shiny silver disco dress with a very short skirt, which she kept on as she re-emerged, smiling her big new smile, with Olaf trailing behind her, arms piled high with bright girly stuff, like a proud grandpa, after almost an hour. It had been an hour of pure joy and delight.

For both of them.

Five

Mama Boo was a pretty decent band after many hard months of touring the Deep South chittlin' circuit and one-nighters in rough and ready road houses. Their sexy, slinky, swampy Southern funk turned out to be irresistible to the younger crowd. They were a solid unit. They wound up in Los Angeles and scored a pretty good gig - house band at Rube's, a little club in Hollywood where they would definitely get noticed. It was a big step up for guys still in their teens. And they were all ready to start.

But then came that death flight.

When Oliver met that geologist, it changed everything for the band. And this is where the story really starts.

Oliver was so shaken up by what had happened, that he decided it was time to shake everything else up, too.

First, he changed the band's name to something utterly weird. He was so convinced by what the geologist had told him, that he wanted to warn everybody. So he did it with the new name.

Fear The Coming New York Earthquake.

Truly bizarre. Shockingly weird. Such a long name. And, since the band were Louisiana boys and had no connection with New York, it was completely inexplicable. But truly memorable.

He cajoled the band into going along with it and, not caring one way or the other so long as they got paid, they said OK.

At the same time, he changed his own stage name to something that sounded more ominous. Oliver Finnegan became Omega Finn.

But the new names were not enough. He wanted to upgrade everything but the music, that sexy, slinky funk that had got them hired in the first place. He wanted the band not only to become Fear The Coming New York Earthquake, but to become something entirely new, a total transformation, a band that was visually unique as well as musically solid, so that they could kick off their new gig at Rube's as if they had sprung out of nowhere.

And to make this all possible - and possibly amazing - he knew exactly who to call.

He called Leo.

Leo was one of the Cajuns, but not in the band. And he was just a flat-out raging genius, an electronics whizz beyond all measure. He had designed games and sold them to the big boys, had invented a coding *slang* and consulted with the Army, and nobody could even imagine the kind of money he was making and had socked away in that hidden palace that he had built on the rim of a canyon on the other side of Malibu. But to give you some idea of his amazing mind, just take a look at his car.

Check it out. A rusted-out old 70s Buick Riviera that nobody would steal, with faded paint of various colors, and streaks of crap that looked like it had been parked under a leaky tin roof and enough birdshit on it that stuff might grow out of it, and in the middle of the roof the *coup de grace*, a patch of actual moss. There were cracked and faded windows so you could not see inside. But they didn't look custom, they just looked fogged up and old.

But yes, they were custom. In fact, the whole rancid old mess was custom. The vehicle was a total con job. The entire Buick was a veneer. When Leo clicked his iPhone and the locks slid back, he opened the door of the old Buick and stepped into a brand new Bentley.

Yes. A Bentley. A brand new Bentley Continental Coupé, custom built in its genius disguise by the astonished and amused engineers of Bentley Motors in the West Midland city of Crewe in England, with Leo in control and all those top notch engineers grinning from ear to ear at the audacity of the crazy commission.

When this apparently shameful piece of disreputable automotive trash finally rolled out of the famous factory and onto the lot, at a cost nobody could even guess at, the entire staff of Bentley Motors came out to laugh and cheer and drink Leo's excellent champagne.

Instead of keys, a special Leo-customized iPhone was handed over to him with much ceremony and he clicked open the doors of this crummy, disgusting, rusted-out husk of a 70s Buick shell and slid into the buttery Andalusian leather seats and birdseye maple dashboard of the pride and joy of English automotive engineering with its lovely leathery new-car smell. When he closed the door, the Bentley simply disappeared and the rusty Buick stood there in its place, in all its shameful, filthy, comical genius.

Leo fluffed up her purring motor, pulled a couple of outrageous donuts on the tarmac, tires smoking, to even louder English cheers, and sped off with four outriders on Harleys - Oliver and the band, flown in specially by Leo for the occasion - to cruise at a stately 70 mph down the M1 Motorway in formation.

And that was just his car.

Leo had left Louisiana for MIT around the time Ollie and crew were learning chords. But they had stayed close. You can take the boy out of the bayou, but you can't take the swamp out of the boy.

He tore through his courses in computer science, was a pimply legend in his freshman year, was cruised by all the tech giants, and after freelancing left and right until he had enough loot to set up on his own, still a teenager, he sold his first video game and quit school to be a professional genius and amateur rumor, already filthy rich.

While the band were coming up slowly, Leo had been zooming up like a rocket. With the metabolism of a hummingbird, he'd been nonstop coding, creating and consulting. But, easily bored, when Oliver suggested collaborating, he jumped at it.

Oliver and the boys hooked up with him the minute they hit L.A. and discovered that he was already richer than shit and living in a Topanga Canyon palace as invisible as his car and impossible to find unless Leo drove you there in his crazy stealth vehicle.

Underground is a term that gets used a lot. Underground music, underground theater and so on, But Leo's place was the real thing. Literally. Under. The. Ground.

Why he did this he could never fully explain. A love of enigma, of being undercover, as he was with the military, or just for the hell of it? Whatever the reason, Leo had dug himself one beautiful hole.

It was on the very crest of the ridge, far up the canyon, on a barely visible dirt track. On the side where you approached it, up the track, it was invisible. You could see only the grassy hilltop. But on the far side, on the side away from prying eyes, it was a palace, wide open to the sky, with terraces and tropical flowers and views for ever. On the far side, there were glorious sunsets and soaring hawks. On the far side you could damn near see China.

The boys moved in. Their transformation was about to begin.

Six

Macumba's first encounter with a flushing toilet bowl was hilarious, if your sense of humor runs to that type of slapstick.

But the most perilous part of her adventure so far, next to nearly drowning in the Rio Negro, had to be the new and dangerous ordeal of learning how to walk on high heels.

The TV was always on in the Manaus dump that she had been brought to, and once she had mastered the pure black magic of the remote switch, she soon chose her favorite show, the 24-hr fashion channel, with a signal stolen from a nearby satellite dish. The old girls preferred the soaps, over which they wept buckets. But Macumba didn't understand a word, was bored stiff, and after glancing at the cartoons, which left her speechless with terror, she saw her very first runway show - Chanel, as it happened - and she was hooked. When one of the women tried to prise the clicker away from her, she bit her. So that was that. Fashion ruled.

Olaf's granddaughter, unknowingly, had bequeathed her a pair of heels along with her Manaus wardrobe, and Macumba became obsessed with mastering them. Every model on every TV fashion runway swished around on stilettos, and so she assumed that the entire female world outside of her Manaus hovel walked around that way, and she was therefore determined to learn how.

Much broken furniture and many scrapes and bruises to herself and to the women around her finally yielded a certain success, and pretty soon she had the TV fashion models' strut down cold, right down to the extravagant butt wiggle with the hand on hip.

She swanned and twirled around the apartment for hours this way, to the great amusement of the old women, not least because apart from the shoes, she was naked, in a plastic tiara.

In Olaf's granddaughter's short shorts and tight tees Macumba was breathtaking. So she was not allowed to wear them. In the seedy quarter of Manaus where she was housed, walking around dressed like that would make her dangerously desirable.

In the six months or so that she had been in the city, she had turned the corner from pretty little girl into the kind of creature that caused grown men to go to confession.

Her scrawny boyish body had lost its angular boniness and her corners had all rounded into subtle curves. She had hit a spurt in height and was now several inches taller than when she arrived, taller than all the women, still skinny and sinewy, but fit, athletic, loose-limbed, and walking tall and regal, like her TV role models.

The old women had to keep her looking as plain as possible just to keep the wolves at bay. Sneakers instead of heels, and definitely nothing tight that showed off her cute little body and long legs.

So, for her daily tutorials with Olaf in English and Portuguese, she would travel to his campus basically in a state of disguise, accompanied by her doting and vigilant old minders; flat shoes, long baggy skirts, a knitted hat pulled over her wild and wiry mop of golden hair and a pair of ugly-housewife sunglasses.

But when she arrived, she would eject this dreary cocoon and butterfly into her real self, her new and gilded self. Off with the drag and on with the motley.

Off came the ugly items, which the old women would catch with whoops as they were thrown at them by the laughing teenager. On would go the heels and the shiny silver super-short mini-dress and only then would old Olaf shamble into the room to watch her swanning around in front of the full-length mirror, a furnace of hormonal teen age.

He would always wait before entering because between the throwing off and the putting on, there would be a few moments of exquisite nudity and, kindly gent though he was, he was still a man.

Girls grow up overnight. One day they're pretty, the very next day they're pretty sexy. This was Macumba's very next day. Olaf knew it and the old women, too. Only Macumba seemed unaware that she had stepped from one to the other. She was still the goofy, playful teenager, the jungle child, more comfortable naked, gabbling to Teetoo like her imaginary brother. But small, elegant gestures and flashes of budding femininity alerted anyone with eyes that she was now no longer merely beautiful, but hopelessly, helplessly gorgeous.

Seven

Leo could do anything. Leo could make anything. Draw it on a napkin and Leo could put it in front of you on a table, on a stage, or in the sky if you wanted it. Is it a bird? Is it a plane? No, it's just young Leo messing with your mind.

Leo's big new thing was holography. He had worked on it in theory while sucking on his pencil in Mama Boo, a kid in short pants, watching a few hologram tricks on TV and thinking, if they could do it, so could he, since he was way smarter than the other kids and was already teaching higher math to his teachers.

Then he worked on it for real at the Massachusetts Institute of Technology, which meant working for the US armed forces. He made holograph tanks so real that soldiers ran from them, and jets so real that airforce pilots had to be stopped from chasing them.

Oliver wanted elephants to jump out from behind the curtain and scatter the audience? No problem. Oliver wanted to be an Elvis impersonator and clone himself a dozen times on the same stage? Piece of cake. So that's what the band became known for. Weird spectacle. In fact the multiple Elvis gag became an audience fave when Fear The Coming New York Earthquake finally started their stint as house band at Rube's. It was all over the music videos the minute Leo figured out how to pull it off, and that's when the wild new name started to get widely known. But it was just a name. And since the band was pulling stunts that were so surreal, it was simply seen as that. Just a wacky handle. Nobody gave it much thought.

And anyway, it was nothing compared with some of Oliver and Leo's stunts. In the middle of one tune, there would be a deep rumbling sound, the band all held their heads in agony, then their heads would explode, showering the crowd with real confetti. Great souvenirs.

If dolphins machine-gunned the crowd, or a plane crashed through the roof or cactus sprouted between the seats, it was just another gag from that nutty band with the impossible holograms, and that name. That incomprehensible but unforgettable name.

Eight

It was Madame Joy who pushed her little Ollie to change his stage name from Oliver Finnegan to Omega Finn. She it was who saw the value of rolling the dice and going whole hog on the voodoo Cajun angle, with a name that made him sound frightening.

The way she saw it, it really didn't matter if there was a damned quake or not. It was the fear of it, the threat of it, that was what mattered. This could be his ticket to fame and fortune, if only he played it right. She had read enough palms and scared enough folks to know the value of looking into a hand and foreseeing terrible trouble, unless another palm was crossed with silver. Hers.

Read the hand. Play the hand.

Madame Joy it was who pressed on them the importance of being known specifically as a Cajun band, with the added witchy vibe of those spooky bayous, the shamans, the spells, the potions, the slight shiver of fear, black magic and voodoo of the Louisiana swamps.

Voodoo. That was the underlying vibe. And Madame made damn sure it always stayed there, looming in the shadows.

When she rode the bus up from Baton Rouge to LA, there was a wild reunion up at Leo's place, the bayou boys and their fairy godmother reunited, the band of crazies together again as one. It was an oddball team to change the world, for sure. But change it they did.

The look that Leo and Oliver devised for Omega Finn was all blue. Blue bodysuit, blue face, hands and feet. Plus a long white wig. It allowed Leo to make him invisible onstage, to project onto him any hologram he wanted. In fact, painted blue with a white wig was the only way anybody outside the team knew Omega Finn. Oliver had simply disappeared. There was now only Omega. And nobody knew what Omega looked like under the blue paint, since he left after every show still painted blue. He had created perfect anonymity for himself. He could walk around totally unrecognized. Without the paint, he was just a guy named Oliver, a friend of the band. A nobody.

After he became so incredibly famous, it was perfect that he was so elusive. It all just happened that way. No real plan. But it played into his hands when the shit hit the fan. And it was about to hit it.

Nine

The next urgent thing on Macumba's plate, literally, was the slow, tedious and annoying acquisition of table manners.

Why on earth would anybody want to use a knife and fork when they had a perfectly good set of fingers? Spoons she got. Every tribe on earth has some kind of spoon. And bowl. You can't pick up liquid with your fingers. But a knife and fork? Ridiculous.

She was having none of them, and the whole company would duck as she would fling them away in frustration at the start of her practical education in polite public demeanor.

But she loved Olaf, and even greater than any hatred of the dreaded implements, was her desire to please him. And so, as with the torturous language lessons she had to suffer every day, she tried to grin and bear it. Well, she didn't try to grin.

Even so, the dinners that Olaf's cook served up for Macumba and the old women were a regular jamboree of rage, tears and hysterical laughter. Olaf tried to be sober and correct, to set a good example at table, but secretly he was loving every crazy moment of the wild exercise, highlights of which were flying food, water fights, and Macumba once standing naked on the table pouring a bowl of potato salad over her head while screaming.

It was at one of these farcical chimpanzee tea-parties that a visiting photographer from Paris showed up and quite by chance changed Macumba's world and, to a lesser extent, that of Paris fashion, too. After meeting the man with the camera, her life came full circle, from those runways on TV to actual runways, from playing it as a game, to earning a fortune at the same game.

That he was smitten goes without saying. He was also staggered, flummoxed, dumbfounded, gob-smacked and knocked on his ass. With food up to her elbows and bits of it sticking to her cheeks, holding her fork like a baby, wearing a teeshirt that said DISCO and her hair tied up with duct tape to keep it out of the soup, he had never seen a creature as beautiful as Macumba.

Ten

Right after Oliver's horrific airplane incident, as soon as he had managed to pull himself together after such a trauma, he had tried to contact the relevant scientific groups, the geologists, the volcano guys and the seismologists, and had even forwarded all the dead man's work to various authorities, but had been either rebuffed politely or openly laughed at. It turned out that the old professor was an outsider in that community and over the years had become regarded as a bit of a nut because of his conviction that New York was in much greater danger than anyone imagined from the tiny, sleepy fault that ran in a perfect horizontal across the city. In fact, the professor had referred to it as the '125th St. Fault', placing it right under Harlem's main drag, home of the Apollo Theater, where Oliver had watched the legendary singer James Brown and met him after the show on one unforgettable night, years before.

But the reaction of the entire seismological community was Yes, yes, we all know about that fault. It's called the Ramapo Fault and yes, it has a branch under New York, but there's nothing going on there and it's being monitored, like faults under Kentucky and Tennessee, and so on. The whole thing was just a big yawn to them.

Oliver discovered that there's a whole web of seismic fault lines under the United States that never get mentioned because they just lie there minding their own business for hundreds of years.

Why the prof had his shorts in a knot over this was a mystery to all concerned, but whatever the reason, Oliver could not shake the man's absolute certainty or forget his mention of some new highly sensitive form of measurement that nobody but he knew about, and which altered the whole picture.

But the old man had become like the boy who cried wolf. Go on about something enough and it just becomes noise. Nobody listens. Nobody cares so long as it doesn't happen, and it didn't happen for several years.

And then it did.

Eleven

The New York earthquake turned out to be a small one, like the dead professor had predicted. But small is relative. In a metropolis as densely packed, as spectacularly vertical and, for the most part, as old and unprepared as Manhattan, any kind of tremor is simply unimaginable and terrifying. Almost as many folks died of heart attacks as did from falling masonry. The terror was total.

Imagine the sound of several million screams, the explosion of a million shattered window and the hail of a billion glass shards pelting down on sidewalks from way up in the sky.

Imagine a stone gargoyle crashing down on a yellow taxi.

Imagine walking down that Sixth Avenue canyon of skyscrapers and feeling the earth tremble underfoot and picturing it all falling down on you.

Imagine being on the hundredth floor of your ultra-luxury condo and getting lurched off your feet as your priceless Sung Dynasty ceramic hits the floor and smashes.

Imagine ruptured gas mains and fires and sirens and an army of walking wounded staggering into Manhattan emergency rooms.

Amazingly few died. It happened early on a Sunday morning. Most folks were in bed, and few subways were running. And it was a weak tremor with no aftershocks. But nobody who was there and awake will forget the absolute horror and the pure nightmare of feeling so utterly helpless and thankful to be alive.

Elevators stuck. Thousands of sleepy people in their nighties and underwear ran down stairwells and into the street. Many fell to their knees and prayed, to hell with acting cool. Dogs howled ceaselessly. And by afternoon, there was looting everywhere and the cops started firing warning shots over people's heads.

In a week, the place was getting back to normal and all main services were running. But the damage was in the billions. Giant insurance companies were talking bankruptcy and everybody was suing the city.

All TV channels across the country and the world were running nonstop eyewitness stories on it. Celebrities with cuts and bruises and attractively placed band-aids were all over the news spouting their near-death sagas, while holding their cute little pet lapdogs.

But bit by bit, and it only took a few days to happen, one name was creeping to the top of all the front-page headlines all over the world and on every TV news broadcast.

The name was Omega Finn.

Overnight, the old interviews in the music press and on old teen rock videos were reprinted and re-broadcast at all hours, nonstop, and translated into every language on earth. Who could ignore a band called Fear The Coming New York Earthquake?

And who was this young singer and front-man Omega Finn, who may be cute and charming, young and skinny and painted blue, with a long white wig, but who must also be kind of terrifying, too, what with that scary name and all, no?

It was wildfire. Oliver and Madame Joy needed to do nothing more than watch, nor could they do more than watch. Social media took over. It was a firestorm of speculation, rumor, flat-out lies and, above all else, fear-mongering. In no time at all there was a genuine, all-consuming dread of a mysterious individual who, alone on planet Earth, had known that this was going to happen, had told everybody who would listen that it was going to happen, had even named his band with that same warning and, many now believed, in a hysterical spiral of conjecture, had maybe even actually *caused* it to happen.

The New York earthquake spawned an instant industry of copycat artists and fakers of every stripe, who claimed they had also predicted this - Earth Quacks is what the media called them. But one by one they were shaken out and crawled back under their rocks and the search was on for the one genuine prophet and possible supernatural being who foresaw all this and who, God help us, may even have made it all happen. Holy shit.

There were two questions the world wanted answered right now. Who the fuck was Omega Finn? Where the fuck was Omega Finn?

Twelve

He was with Leo, and well hidden.

As was the whole band and Madame Joy. Plus the handful of groupies without whom the band refused to go into hiding.

And hiding it was. Total. A commando unit of Navy Seals with satellite uplinks and very well trained dogs might eventually find Leo's place, but even that was not guaranteed. It was un-findable. Whenever Leo drove his rusty old lump of Buick scrap metal with the Bentley inside, from Malibu, along Pacific Coast Highway, then turned away from the ocean and up into Topanga Canyon, it was like he was simply erased.

The illegal Mexican laborers who had built his place never really knew where they were. The civil engineer who designed it never knew where it was gong to be built. The contractors who hauled the materials up the dirt track never knew what they were for, and the Caterpillar operator who dug the hole was told it was a mining operation. After it was finished, if you stood in front of it, looking right at it, you still wouldn't be able to see it. It was invisible, just a part of the hill.

But inside? Imagine a duplex penthouse with sunset views forever clear across the Malibu mountains to the sea from terraces on the hidden side, covered in tropical bougainvillea and frangipani, a kitchen and a chef that both belonged on a TV show, and a superb wine cellar cut into the cool canyon earth.

But right now, nobody was discussing the view or the flowers or the food and wine served up by the chef who was very well-paid to see nothing and say nothing

Everybody was freaked. Even Madame Joy. At first. Every TV channel had Omega Finn on it and was talking about the band whose name had the world rigid with fear. Why had they changed their name? How did they know this would happen? Who were these guys? What exactly were Cajuns anyway? And why the name Omega, the last letter of the Greek alphabet? What did it signify? The end? The end of what? End of the world? Did his powers go as far as actually *causing* the quake? Could the insurance companies sue him?

On it went, nonstop questions tumbling after each other in a mad cascade of blather and bullshit and genuine fear.

It didn't take much digging to link Omega Finn to Mama Boo, the story of a nice Louisiana boy transformed into a teenage Satan.

The poor neighbors down in the Mama Boo bayous locked their doors and moved to nearby relatives as the place was overrun with reporters yammering away in every language and not very careful where they stepped. Gators got a few stragglers before they wised up and set up in Baton Rouge or some other place a little less liquid.

Omega Finn sightings became a minor industry and a kind of sport. Social media was choked with guys painted blue claiming to be Omega, from criminal con artists trying to make a quick buck, to frat boys playing it for laughs, then a meme series of chipmunks, meerkats, hippos and cats holding up signs saying 'I am Omega Finn'.

The only photos of the real Omega that surfaced were of him onstage painted blue with a white wig looking perfectly mysterious.

Up in Leo's canyon hideout, it took a good week of trying to get their heads around the whirlwind they had sown, before they all started to calm down enough to think about what in hell they were actually going to do now, and how to proceed.

Should they come clean about all this and let everybody know that Oliver was simply in the right place at the right time with the professor on the plane? Should they apologize for accidentally scaring the shit out of everybody? Should they downplay the whole Cajun bayou angle? Try to sell themselves as regular folks caught in a misunderstanding? Should they try to disappear and hope that it blew over and everybody would just forget about them?

One thing was sure. They could not stay hidden. Some people knew where Leo lived and, even though he assured them he had no idea where the band was, how long would it be before they came up the hill to look for the band themselves?

They had to emerge soon and have their story straight, stay in control and not get buried by this avalanche of insane media. As usual, it was Madame Joy who decided what to do. She delivered her verdict on the mountain top, literally, wise old Buddha that she was.

She had just one piece of advice. Go Big.

Thirteen

It was mutual.

Macumba was just as taken with the French photographer as he with her. She liked the way he made her look in the photos he shot. But even more than that, she felt at ease with him and trusted him around her, clothed or naked, and did not feel like he was about to jump on her, the way she felt around Olaf's male students when they caught sight of her and stood there hyperventilating, before being shooed off by the old women.

No, there was something about this guy that was different from them and she pretty soon figured out what it was. He was gay. He was just like a couple of the boys in her village who were the same way and whom she loved very much. Nothing was said. The words were simply not there. But they were not needed. The two formed an understanding and fell a little bit in love in that special way.

His name was Fabien, and nobody could dress her the way he did, the way he would drape a bit of something just so, or even make her look cool in some piece of tat she didn't even like, or didn't think she liked until he placed it on her, just so.

His accented English was a problem, but she got the gist of it, and when he asked Olaf if Macumba could please move in with him into his campus apartment, a far more pleasant arrangement than the dump she was currently occupying, the old prof agreed. He knew Fabien, he understood the situation exactly, and approved.

Macumba was ecstatic.

The old women were not.

Macumba was to them a religious figure, a blossoming juju woman with powers that she was yet to reveal, but which were there, innate, and would emerge some day, whether the girl wanted them to or not. Maybe it would be in a moment of danger to herself or to those close to her, but it would come out. It must. The women had felt this before, with others, and they were always right. But they had never felt it as strongly as with this girl, this living vessel of magic.

The situation was indeed very delicate. The women had sought out Olaf only in order to communicate with Macumba, which they now did, but could only do through him, and he was happy for this to continue. In fact he was making them part of a study he was doing for the university.

So they were all important to each other and Olaf did not want to rock the boat.

But Macumba was developing in ways the women could never understand. To them she was still the golden baby goddess on the floating log, her destiny to become a voodoo priestess.

To Olaf and Fabien and to Macumba herself, the future looked very different. To them the future looked more like the 24-hour fashion channel. To them, the future looked more like Paris.

Fabien had already persuaded her to remove the little white bone from her lower lip and had it made into an earring that she wore for a while until she was bored with it, as the little hole under her lower lip started to close and heal over and disappear. In her mind she was already moving from the jungle to the possibility of Paris and maybe even life as a model. Fabien had sent shots of her to various people and they had created something of a buzz. They all wanted to know more about this exquisite golden-skinned creature, while in Manaus she was simply devouring every scrap she could find about Paris fashion, the world of runways and the rest of that promised land she had first glimpsed on the TV in the slum.

I knew Fabien a little. I had written about a gallery show of his, and we had stayed in touch. So his part in this story and all that happened later came directly from his retelling of it to me.

Anyway, Macumba moved in with him and told the women, via Olaf, that it was simply a nicer place to sleep because it stank less and there were no rats. So they were pushed to accept.

But they did not accept. They were not stupid. They knew that they were losing their hold on this girl and that their plans for her were failing fast, thanks to this French interloper.

So they decided to do something about it.

Fourteen

Madame Joy's advice was simplicity itself. Do nothing.

She made them all grasp the fact that this worldwide shit-storm they had accidentally set off was a dream come true. The world had handed them the greatest possible gift. They should run with it.

Own it. Turn notoriety into money.

She put it this way. The world may be mystified. But they were not. Nobody knew what was happening. But they did. They were the only ones on the planet who knew what had really happened. So why let anybody else know that? Why explain? Why calm everybody down? Why try to stop the fear?

Everybody was scared of them? Great. Why change that?

In fact, they should do the opposite. They should fan the flames, deepen the mystery, stoke the madness. And to do this, all they had to do was to stay silent. Explain nothing. Make everybody even more scared. Make Omega Finn even more of a bogeyman. If folks wanted to see the Omega Finn story as a nice young Cajun singer transformed by dark forces into a master of disaster, then let them run with it and hope it kept them awake at night.

Like the lady said... go big.

But first, they had to disperse. Lighten up. Be more nimble. The band went to Mexico in a big helicopter, to a grand villa above Oaxaca. Nobody there knew who they were And the groupies loved it.

Oliver and Madame Joy stayed with Leo, to make plans and get creative. Three people could easily get picked up in a chopper very fast, if it came to that. And Leo had technical capabilities up on that ridge that a James Bond villain would be proud of. Whatever idea they came up with, Leo could design it, edit it, bounce it off a satellite and have it show up anywhere in the world as a hologram, a silkscreen or on everybody's phone screen. Propaganda 101.

So, every day for a week they would scratch their heads all day then sit out on the terrace with a beer, watch those thermonuclear Southern California sunsets, and figure out how to do it. How to scare the shit out of everybody. How to make a fortune out of it. How to get away with it. And one thing above all. How to go big.

Fifteen

She needed her stuff.

Like all teenage girls who love dressing up, Macumba had built a small hill of girly crap during the months she had been in the slum. And, needless to say, she could not *possibly* live without any of it after moving in with Fabien. So Olaf, soft touch that he was, had been persuaded to drive over and pick it all up. She had pulled a face. A pleading teenage face. She was learning fast.

He had a tough time finding the place among the warren of red dirt streets rutted out with the rains and barely driveable. When he finally shambled up the dirt path to the front door he heard a loud argument going on inside. The women were yelling colorful and filthy-sounding oaths that Olaf had never heard before, and, smiling to himself, he made a mental note to add a few of them to his jungle dictionary, later.

He stood by the door and lit his pipe, reluctant to walk in on this raging hubbub, chuckling at some of the obscene locutions that were flying around. And it was a good job he did stand there. In between the curses and obscenities, he gleaned the gist of the uproar.

They were going to kidnap the girl.

That, they were all agreed on. The violent differences were only about when they were going to do it. A few weekends from now? This coming weekend?

He stood there and let the argument play out, extinguishing his pipe, lest the smell of it give him away. When he was sure it was all settled, he tiptoed away, got back in his car and bounced it back along the same muddy ruts, back to the downtown district, the campus, and the mercifully paved roads.

He had heard enough. They were planning to snatch her two weeks from now, on a Sunday, when the campus would be deserted.

He went to his study, flopped into his armchair, felt suddenly very old, poured two stiff whiskeys, dialed Fabien's number and asked him to come on over.

Sixteen

The album they made was called *The End*. The artist Omega Finn. We know that now. but when it came out it was a complete mystery.

To say it was a hit would be a joke. It earned more money than the gross national budget of small countries. But more of that later.

The genius was partly in the logo design, plain black with five white horizontal lines stacked one above the other, the sign that came to be known as the Pentagraph. But no name. A complete mystery.

The genius was partly in the music - a dark, brooding, sexy, very danceable, swampy funk of the New Orleans voodoo school. A groove that never let up, a cool sly cosmic slot you could lay down and inwardly evaporate to, or make love to, or dance all night to.

The genius was partly in the lyrics. There were very few, all about being oblique and invisible and fascinating and hard to unravel, but controlling and quietly masterful and so on. It was an ode to vagueness, teasing, slightly sadistic and reassuring all at the same time. It meant whatever you wanted it to. And it was sexy as hell.

But the true genius, the thing that made it historic, lay in the rumors that surrounded the release. That is what started the fuss.

First, there was a barrage of advertising. The End Is Coming, The End Is Near and so on, in all the places you would expect to see regular music ads. Nothing special. Just an ad campaign. But then...

But then, alarmingly, on every screen you could imagine, on TVs, laptops, car dashboards, your own phone, everywhere around the world, at the same moment, interrupting all programs for a few long seconds, then gone with no explanation - the Pentagraph.

Holy shit. What *was* that? Nobody knew. Nobody. The world went nuts. Literally, the world. This was a global hack. A spectacular hack. It was generally agreed to be impossible. But it had really happened. Everywhere on Earth at the same moment? Who could do that? Was it Government? Was it the Russians? The North Koreans?

It was Leo. It was just young Leo messing with your mind.

The Internet crashed. Several times. TV pundits on the Left and the Right accused each other. Motions in Congress. Questions in Parliament. Social media went ape-shit. For the usual conspiracy rogues it was playtime. For the usual conspiracy suckers it was a banquet. So much bullshit to believe. So much bullshit to spread. Paradise for morons. An exponential holocaust of gullibility and bullshit.

The genius, part two, was the silence that followed.

Madame, once again guiding the guided missile, made sure that the rumor pump was pumping at full crank by allowing only rumor. No fact. No revelation. No explanation. No coming clean to the world. Because it was she who was controlling the rumors.

She and Leo gathered together a gang of media influencers. These kids had no idea they were even working with each other, and no clue as to who was influencing the influencers. Madame Joy got a priceless overnight education in social media manipulation from Leo. Who better to teach her how the system works and how to work it? Who better to game the game than the gamer deluxe?

Picture it. First, the horrific New York earthquake. Then silence. Then the avalanche of interest in a band called Fear The Coming New York Earthquake. Then silence. Then the global search for Omega Finn, the bogeyman. Then silence. Then the ad campaign that says The End Is Coming. Then silence. Then the release of the mystery nameless album with the Pentagraph logo. Then the same Pentagraph appears on every screen everywhere on earth, with no name and no explanation. Then silence.

Then the rumors.

And the rumors coming from all the trusted young social stars are saying that it's all connected. Yes! All of it! Connected! OMG!

That mystery no-name music with the Pentagraph? It's called *The End*! And it's by Fear The Coming New York Earthquake! And the lead singer is Omega Finn, the guy who predicted the earthquake, and may have even caused it! It's all connected! Oh my God!

Prophesy. Catastrophe. Voodoo. Rock 'n' roll.

Oh. My. Freaking. God.

Seventeen

He was a prince.

Noble, fearless, intrepid, resourceful, loyal, intelligent, loving, and bright green.

Teetoo was a most excellent lizard. An aristocrat among reptiles. And in his antics he was a constant source of amusement to the entire company, whatever the company. Raised by Macumba since poking his green head out of an egg, he had a great affinity for humans and an endless tolerance for their foibles, though he could barely believe some of them.

Swatting flies he could understand. Failing to eat them? Weird.

But his attitude was basically 'more for me', and he was not shy in getting his share. He ate his weight. Daily. Or so it seemed. He was never not hunting. Bugs. Every type of bug. It was his total obsession and he was an athlete at it. An Olympian. Gold medalist. He represented his country at bug eating, He ate bugs for Brazil.

His motto: if it flies, eat it. If it crawls, eat it. If it stands still for too long, eat it. If it's smaller than your head, eat it.

Teetoo had survived the flood, the log, the treehouse, the hungry monkeys, the yellow snakes, the red macaws, the canoe ride to the big riverboat, the riverboat to Manaus, the river rats, the captain's cat, the passengers' kids, the kids' dog, the wobbly gangplank, the bumpy taxi, the Manaus slum, the slum rats, the slum cats, the slum kids, the slum kids' dogs.... all of this. But finally he was confronted with something far more perilous. He was threatened with the loss of his refuge, his home, his habitat, his living quarters, the center of his entire lifestyle.

They were planning to weave Macumba's cloud of wild golden hair into neat cornrows. And Macumba's hair was where he lived.

Inseparable is a word that is bandied about a lot. But Macumba and Teetoo were literally inseparable. One lived in the other. The puffy mushroom cloud of pale hair that glowed gold in the sunlight was not only Macumba's crowning glory. It was his house.

She had shoved him up in there right after he was hatched, to hide him from brothers and sisters and pet monkeys. And for a lizard, straight out of the egg, it felt just right. He figured that's what a lizard did and that's how a lizard hid.

When he poked his head out of her golden thatch, he was no bigger than a small green gemstone and looked just as cute, like a piece of jewelry, like an emerald. But an emerald that blinked.

Teetoo was the village word for jewel and since that's what he was, that's what they called him. All the kids wore something. She wore him.

Teetoo never grew big. He remained tiny, fit in her hand, ran up her arm and hid in her hair. And that's how they grew up together. Inseparable. And here they still were in Manaus, still together.

He had survived every kind of threat to his life, but a lizard had no answer for a comb. Faced with the demands of fashion and the prospect of an actual hairdo, what was a lizard to do?

This was a problem as knotty for Macumba as it was for Teetoo. He had never known another home, and she had never had to think twice about where to put him.

Teetoo's solution was the same as Madame Joy's. Do nothing.

He did nothing. He just went off on one of his safaris, hunting small game, and when he got back, with a bellyful of bugs and a look of sleepy satisfaction, he just took up his usual place on her head, front and center. His house had changed a lot, he had to admit. The new cornrows had made it more open-plan now with no roof. Breezy. But it was still perfectly warm up there and the view was much better. So he just wrapped his tiny claws around the usual few strands of gold, and took his nap.

When Macumba moved around, he just hung on as usual, it was second nature, but now it was more like cruising in a convertible, and he'd always been a bit of a show-off.

The photograph that Fabien took of Macumba with her bare golden shoulders, her brand new golden cornrows, looking into the camera with her pale amber eyes and with a little emerald lizard on her head went straight to Paris and straight onto the cover of *Vogue.*

Eighteen

Up in Topanga Canyon it was time for the plotters to exhale.

It had been a frantic few weeks after the quake. Getting the music done had been the easy part. This was a working band, so they just laid down that sexy groove and cut old tunes to fit with new words, hired studio studs to polish it, and recorded them remotely.

It was the hack that took all the brains and hard work. The hack was Oliver's greatest idea and Leo's greatest accomplishment. Getting those five white lines on every screen everywhere at the same moment beat Santa's trick of delivering all the gifts on the same night. Nobody could figure out how Leo had done it. The hack left the world in a state of shock and primed the pump for Madame's next inspired idea.

"Boys," she said, "We're goin' back to the future."

The album was released in all the main streaming formats, but she said they should also release it on CDs and make a big fuss about that.

Compact Discs were an out-of-style format, but she needed an object, an actual object to imbue with the magic Omega voodoo dust, one that was small enough to be slipped into a pocket or a purse. CDs were perfect The CD *itself* should be the center of attention. Not the music. Yes. The actual piece of plastic that the CD came in. The music could be streamed. But the CD would be sold as something way bigger.

It would be sold as an amulet. A charm. Not the kind that brings good luck. The opposite. The kind that wards off *bad* luck. Much more scary. Much more powerful. Much more voodoo.

That little square of black plastic with the white Pentagraph on it could be the key to massive money. The CD itself was pure bullion.

Oh, you could wear your cross, your Star of David or whatever floats your boat. But make sure you also have that CD in your house. Or your car. Or your pocket. Or your purse. Or else.

And the more of them you buy, the less your chance of bad luck. That was the final detail, the final ka-ching of the cash register. What a sales pitch! Buy your luck. The more you buy, the safer you are.

And it worked! The CD became the most desired object on the planet. Diamonds were mere luxuries. But an object that kept bad luck away? Priceless. Essential. A must have.

Nineteen

It was in the middle of a storm that they came for Macumba. Clatters of thunder that set the dogs off, sheets of white lightning, black skies hurling rain that bounced high off the roads, the roads turned to rivers, buses stranded, cars starting to float, the jungle again reminding the city that it was not welcome.

Like drowned rats, the four women made it to the campus, holding on to each other against the wild whips of wind. They pounded on the professor's door but there was no reply. They staggered across a quadrangle and banged on Fabien's door with the same result. The place was deserted. It was a Sunday, on an urban campus, and all the students lived in town. And it was a huge storm. They had no choice but to wait, sopping wet, huddled in the corridor, checking their equipment. Ropes to tie her up, duct tape to shut her up, a rolled-up carpet in which to wrap her up and carry her to the boat, and a little box for the little lizard.

That's where the cops found them after the rain, fast asleep and snoring in a puddled clump on the floor outside Fabien's door, right where Olaf said they would be, with all the kidnap evidence in a pile, ropes, duct tape, carpet, box, and five tickets for the trip back up the Rio Negro to their village, where they could knock some sense into the silly girl who had magic powers and didn't want them.

They were treated very gently under the circumstances. Kidnap, abduction, involuntary detention, etc., could add up to serious time in a roach-riddled shit hole in the bowels of an old colonial dungeon where rat was on the menu only if you bribed the right guard.

They were tried quietly without a jury and royally scared by the judge, whose sole aim was to give them nightmares for the next few years if they even dreamed of coming back to Manaus. And after a couple of nights in the same shit hole they almost spent the rest of their lives in, they were put on a boat, knowing how lucky they were.

The judge and the professor watched their boat pull away from the quay and sail upstream back to their village.

Then the two old pals and conspirators went to dinner together.

Twenty

Manaus has its moments.

In the old downtown, there are parks, boulevards, statues and fountains, a cute painted cathedral, and the famous old opera house, world class and so surreally out of place here in the Amazonian jungle and so spectacular that you have to pinch yourself.

But the only way to feel really grand in Manaus is to leave it. In style. On a very grand vessel called the *Grand Amazon,* for a week-long cruise up the Rio Negro in a private cabin with a river view.

As the four bedraggled old girls were put on the riverboat, led there in handcuffs by armed police, the better to scare the shit out of them, and pointed back upstream whence they came, Fabien was introducing Macumba to the joys of chilled champagne, careful to make sure it was only a tiny sip at a time, on the same big river, in very different circumstances indeed, leaning over the rail of the *Grand Amazon* and feeling the quiet rumble of the giant marine engines through the soles of their happy bare feet.

Fabien had money. Not crazy money, but enough to live well on, and to go pretty much wherever he pleased, and do so in style. And he knew people. In Paris he was a top fashion shooter, welcome everywhere he wanted to be, but he wanted to be with the kind of people who don't care about fashion. Writers, readers, wanderers, and white haired old Norwegians who know the jungle well. His idea of a good time was to paddle with Olaf up some steamy creek, taking shots of head-dresses, and burning leeches off his ankles.

He had shot his share of tribal elders and tattooed children, in the service of anthropology, then gone back to Paris or Rome to make big bucks in the world of fashion. Never had he dreamed the two worlds could meet. Then came Macumba.

As he looked at her now, dressed in the simple white linen dress he had bought for her on one of those Manaus boulevards, he found her as surreally unlikely as an opera house in the jungle, and more lovely than any supermodel he'd met. And he'd met them all.

The hair stylist Fabien had found online to make some sense out of Macumba's mushroom cloud of golden hair, had found stuff in it that she'd never seen in hair before, a lifetime of bits of jungle she could not identify. Mercifully, there was no lizard shit. Teetoo was meticulous about keeping his nest clean, a general lizard habit that the stylist was unaware of, as she was unaware that a lizard had been living in there in the first place. Fabien had told Macumba that maybe she should not mention the lizard detail, for fear the young woman might run out of the room screaming.

It took an entire day. The process was painstaking, the stylist was meticulous, the patient was patient, the result was spectacular.

As the exhausted woman stepped back one last time to admire her gold cornrows, Teetoo jumped off a table onto Macumba, ran up her arm and sat on her head. Macumba reached up to touch him gently, and was still smiling as the woman fell on the floor.

The *Vogue* cover photo was taken a few minutes later, after the poor stylist had been revived with a stiff brandy and had left for home almost at a run, still freaked, but mollified by the week's wages she had earned in a day, happily shelled out by Fabien.

The photograph that changed so many lives was quite casually shot, with no set-up, no lighting, no stylist, no make-up artist and no instructions to the model. But it was no accident.

Fabien knew a killer shot when he saw one. And he saw it as the golden girl turned towards him at that golden hour before sunset, golden light pouring in through the window, her golden shoulders bare, and raised those pale amber eyes to the lens as Teetoo blinked.

Click. Click. Click. Fashion history.

And here she was again at another golden hour before sunset, a flute of champagne in her hand, gazing across the big river as the sun set, turning the Rio Negro into a river of pure gold, with Fabien thinking that the old women were right. Macumba was magic.

The cruise had been magic too, and was headed back downstream, just as the upstream riverboat with the four women sitting among the chickens and pigs looked up, along with the other passengers, as the majestic *Grand Amazon* glided by with its lucky guests, among them a slim Frenchman with a golden skinned beauty in a white linen dress, sipping champagne, a few meters and a world away.

Twenty One

Where were you when President Kennedy was shot?

That's the famous question members of an earlier generation would ask each other, knowing that each person would recall the moment vividly. These days the question might well be asked of where you were when you first held the CD of *The End*.

That's how big a deal it was.

The question is very specific. It does not refer to the moment you first heard the music, or saw on TV the lines around the block waiting to get their hands on a copy, all over the world, limited as they were to two per person in those first weeks.

No. It refers to the moment you first actually *held* it, the CD itself, the amulet, the charm, the talisman, the totem, the fetish, the juju that Madame Joy had sprinkled with her fairy dust, or her devil dust. When did you first hold in your bare hands the small square of black plastic with the white Pentagraph on it and the CD inside?

They might add, '...and did you not feel a sense of relief?'

The CD of *The End* got churned out and snapped up by the million, eventually by the billion, for its power as a voodoo object, an amulet against bad luck. Soon it seemed like everyone on the planet owned one, or a few, or a lot. They jangled in bundles from rear-view mirrors in the poorer neighborhoods, and in the fancier ones, entire walls were covered in them, swimming pools lined with them, because you can't be too careful, can you? Bad luck is all around us, just waiting to pounce on you, rich or poor. The Fear ruled. And Omega and Madame stoked the fires that fueled The Fear.

Oh, and don't even think of pirating a copy. The juju juice only works if the CD was bought from Omega's company, The Final Corporation. They had ways of instantly detecting a fake copy, and there were rumors of people being dragged out of their houses and beaten up over this, and who cares if the rumors are true or not? A fake copy will simply piss off Omega Finn personally, and you don't want the master of disaster mad at you, do you, kids?

No, you freaking well don't.

Twenty Two

The Fear didn't arrive full-blown. It took a while to scare folks stiff. At first it was just Madame Joy feeding the social networks the kind of rumor they lapped up like honey; that Omega Finn was a gypsy prince from Albania, or Romania or even scarier Transylvania, or that he was found floating in a Louisiana swamp like Moses, or he was a Russian aristo raised by wolves, or that his skin really *was* bright blue because he was a shape-shifting alien from the planet Orion.

But it was the Pentagraph that nailed it shut. Those five lines were rumored to be the lines of the five-pointed star, the ancient pentagram, beloved of devil-worshipers, and that they were altered, in a Satanic rite, to work for Omega alone. Pentagram to Pentagraph. Simple story. For simple minds. It was believed. It sealed the deal. Omega was now magic.

After Leo's famous global hack, the Pentagraph did not raise its head again until later that year in hurricane season in the Deep South, where they brace themselves for disaster for the whole month of September in Tornado Alley. In that swath of Texas and Kansas, a big twister came through and ripped the heart out of an entire small town. It was the dreaded 'big one', that worst-case scenario that the storm chasers talk about but which seldom shows up. This one did.

The devastation was spectacular. A perfect tornado. Nothing was left. Just weeping folks emerging from their storm shelters, stumbling around and looking for something that might be left of their house, or street, or town. But it was all gone. All. An entire country town was scattered like birdseed over the next ten miles. Walls, roofs, floors, cars, cows, everything, all gone. The first TV images were horrifying. And at that soon-to-be-notorious moment, all TV screens went dark, coast to coast, and for the next ten seconds, the five white lines of the Pentagraph faded up, hung there silently, then faded out.

What did it mean? That Omega Finn had caused this tornado? That he could prevent tornadoes? Or what? *Or what?*

No answer. Only silence. And that's when it really began. The Fear.

The minute Leo hacked that tornado newscast with the Pentagraph, it was all over, game, set and lighted match. Omega *owned* the occult.

After that, whenever there was a major disaster on the news, with the exception of terrorist attacks, the Pentagraph would fade up and hang there, with all the networks hacked at the same moment. How was it done? Nobody knew. Just young Leo messing with your mind.

At a certain velocity an object escapes Earth's gravity. At a certain saturation, a liquid creates crystals. And rumor becomes fact.

There was no further need for Madame to feed the rumor mill. It churned by itself. She merely nudged it. She did try to make clear that the Pentagraph was only a reminder that bad luck was around the corner, *not* as a suggestion that Omega could cause bad luck. But nobody listened. The CD of *The End* became a rabbit's foot against misfortune. So many metric tons of CDs were sold, that global plastic production had to be ramped up, and Oliver started to get insanely rich.

And he was a rock star too, lest we forget. None of the scare tactics would have meant a thing if the music wasn't great, and it was. The band, The Fear, was a great rock unit, with cool riffs and a pedigree of the blues, and Oliver's knack for menace in the lyrics made their slinky, sexy, bluesy danceable rock just irresistable.

They were good-looking lads, too. Young, chill, easy-going, a little scary with their voodoo vibe, but definitely the new rock royalty. It became super cool to be Cajun. Like being a pirate or riverboat gambler or a gunslinger, being Cajun got to be the new chic. Cajun this, Cajun that, the look, the clothes, the diamond-in-the-rough, don't-give-a-shit, ramblin', gamblin' attitude, all summed up in their cars and motorbikes. Dragsters and dirt bikes. No fancy brands. Stuff you build yourself was the thing. Style your wheels and your clothes yourself, that was the new style. It was a healthy left-turn from the brand names and the bling and showing off your money. Madame Joy was right. We're Cajuns and proud of it. Tattoos and earrings and motor oil under our fingernails. Fixing stuff up. We like things a little battered so we can put our stamp on 'em. It was back to cheap and nasty and punk and fun. And everybody could afford it. Get real. Be yourself. Wake up your inner bayou, wade in your inner swamp.

Thrift shops, yard sales, second-hand, beat-up, these were the new cool. Smooth was out. Rough was in. Punk was back. Outrage and scandal. Fun. Screw the labels. Our favorite brand? *We are*, baby!

Twenty Three

Advertising agencies are peopled by the smartest guys on earth and, they say, some of the biggest assholes, often in the same body.

Oh, some of them feel a wee bit guilty about persuading suckers to spend their hard-earned wages on things they don't need and can't afford. But most of them don't give a shit.

Mona Callan didn't give a shit. She ran the hottest ad agency in New York. She was exactly what the crazy Omega Finn zoo lacked. A very smart reptile.

They hired Mona Callan as CEO of The Final Corporation.

Madame Joy hated her. Oliver hated her. Leo hated her. But they all agreed on the need. Madame, Ollie and Leo couldn't run a big business to save their lives, and the Omega Finn organization was now very big business indeed. And so, as long as Mona never went near the creative side of things or public relations, she would be perfect to ride herd on the con artists and intellectual property thieves who were starting to besiege the Omega Finn fun factory. Mona did not give one shit about creativity. Or customers. She just liked cracking the whip and making money. That's what she was good at and that's what she was hired to do.

Omega Finn had become global and massive overnight. They knew he would be big. But they were unprepared for the tsunami of money and fame that rolled over them and nearly drowned them.

To run things, Leo's lawyer had set up the company that Oliver named The Final Corporation. This is what Mona was hired to run.

She was one hot woman, too. Tall, athletic, fit, mid-40s, with severely cut bottle blonde hair and two big black dobermans. They went everywhere with her. Yes, even there. And the message was clear. Fuck with me and you're dogmeat.

Mona hired three lieutenants, three killers. Steiner, killer lawyer, Di Stefano, killer financier, and Katsu, killer security chief and the one *actual killer*, ex-yakuza, covered in tattoos, with three black belts that were not for holding up his pants. He scared the shit out of everyone.

The Gang of Four is what Oliver called them. The Gang of Four. The Four Whores of the Apocalypse.

Twenty Four

Fast forward. A couple of years. That's all it took.

With Mona Callan and the Gang of Four running the Final Corporation and Oliver, Madame Joy and Leo coming up with the ideas, Omega Finn had become almost a world religion based on The Fear. His worshippers called themselves the Finnies, and a bleak bunch of black-clad goths they were, too, millions of them worldwide, pushy, scary, threatening violence if you didn't believe in Omega's power, adding millions more to the cult and to the faith.

Money poured in like a tide from all over the world and turned a little rock band into one of the wealthiest corporations on the planet, with franchises selling every kind of merchandise you can imagine from clothing to toys to wallpaper, a fragrance called Fear, a magazine called The End, tattoo parlors, themed cruises, nightclubs, an online store, a Shanghai hotel, an Omega Finn casino going up in Vegas.

New music was released at a steady pace, a cool new tune here and there, just to keep it all funky and to remind everybody that, above all, Omega Finn was a rockstar and the band was great. But money-wise, the music side of things had become almost a sideshow. The main thing now had become the voodoo, the juju, The Fear.

And The Fear was kept at full pitch by two principal things: the scary Omega Finn concerts and the dreaded Pentagraph.

The Pentagraph. Such a simple thing with which to torture the minds of a world of frightened people.

Any catastrophe, an airplane crash, a major flood, a forest fire, an oil spill, an earthquake, any great disaster not associated with terrorism, is followed on the TV news by a ten second shot of the Pentagraph. A silent image. Hanging there. Like a tombstone.

It just sits there, silently, five silent white lines on a black background on every screen, everywhere, just like the cover of that first CD, without comment or sound, as a reminder of what bad luck awaits anybody, at any moment. The added implication that Omega Finn might have actually caused the disaster himself is always denied vehemently by The Final Corporation, but denied in such a way that nobody entirely believes the denial. The Fear grows.

Twenty Five

Fast forward that same couple of years in Macumba's life.

Paris. Rome. Tokyo. London. Berlin. New York, anywhere high fashion rules at any moment, there she is, ruling.

Macumba had been the world's #1 top supermodel from the moment she arrived in Paris. It was instant and unanimous.

Stepping out of that First Class cabin with Fabien, at the end of her first ever plane ride from the steaming jungle city of Manaus to the chill of the Paris Charles de Gaulle airport Terminal One, she walked into a blinding wall of paparazzi and a blaze of publicity that never really stopped from that moment on.

Fabien's world-famous shot of her with Teetoo perched on her head was the cover of French *Vogue* on the day she arrived, and all that day the magazine was shoved in her face for her to sign, which befuddled her completely because not only did she not understand what an autograph was, she was still learning how to write.

She could write 'Macumba', but that was about all. Olaf had taught her to do that, knowing that she would soon have to sign a contract, a passport, an Arrival slip at the airport, a Visa receipt, a bank account, a lease, all the things you take for granted unless you are raised in the jungle by a family with bones in their lower lips.

One scandal that Fabien and Olaf wanted to avoid right at the start was the world's most famous model signing her name with an *X*, hence the painfully practiced and awkwardly executed signature.

She could barely speak English, so interviews could be avoided with a PR release explaining her wish to remain private, thereby making her even more mysterious and fascinating to the public. But an *X*? No. So at least she could sign her name. Her signature was potential scandal enough as it was. It was all capital letters and looked like a baby had written it.

In fact a baby *had* written it. Macumba was a social infant. The stylish young woman who had been introduced to the President of France on the TV had, just a year earlier, been wiping her cute little bottom with a big leaf, in the stream that was her village toilet.

But her childish signature, when it first came to light, boosted her fame even more. It was punk. It was fuck-you. It was interpreted as her way of being primitive, wild, and of thumbing her nose at society. It made her an idol of the young urban kids, on a pure matter of style. But it was also seen among the intelligentsia as her way of identifying, as a girl of color, with the *banlieusards*, the immigrants in the 'banlieus', the slums that surround Paris at a safe distance, the black and brown masses ignored by the rich and well-fed. She became one of their own, and her awkward, punkish signature became their meme, their logo.

Every single thing worked in her favor and nothing was planned. From the babyish illiterate signature, which started to appear as graffiti on walls and teeshirts, to her way of answering all questions with a 'Yes' or a 'No' or a 'Maybe' in English, accompanied by her famous sweet and mysterious smile. In fact she came to be referred to as YesNoMaybe in the press, or even as YNM, the ultimate mark of fame in France, to be known by your initials alone. In fact Yes, No and Maybe were the only words she could say without much trouble, still in the process of learning basic English, forget about French, and were her simple defense against not having understood what was being asked when a microphone was shoved in her face.

Her exquisitely beautiful face.

Macumba's beauty was of a rarity and perfection that made her seem like she was almost from another planet. She was so much more uniquely pretty than any of the other top models, that there was no jealousy. They were all just as floored by her as the average girl in the street, all of whom loved her too. And little Macumba was such a delight with her goofy awkwardness and her genuine modesty and halting speech, making her adorable mistakes while trying so hard to speak English and a little French and getting them mixed up and laughing about it, that even the most acid-tongued bitch in the fashion world would only want to take her under her wing and help her make her stumbling way in the world.

Macumba was simply adored by everyone.

And everyone was very protective of her as soon as they heard her story, the Macumba Miracle, the naked little girl on a log who did not even know where she was from, nor anybody who even spoke her language, yet who was now the most famous girl on Earth.

Twenty Six

There wasn't *only* The Fear. There was a good helping of fun, too.

Omega-mania, Cajunmania, whatever they were calling it this week, was not *only* a cult of fear, it was also a good laugh, too. Kids who could not give a shit about luck, and laughed at The Finnies, were having a blast just with the slinky, sexy music from this band of bayou rockers.

There were two distinct cultures of Omega Finn. The Finnies and the Funnies.

The Finnies were the Goths, the nasty, scary, serious disciples of Omega the prophet, the master of disaster. These were the guys who filled the stadiums at the scary concerts - which we'll get to later - and beat up anybody else who tried to get in. Black was the color and scary was the style. Druids and zombies, satanists, vampires, the unsmiling and the undead. There were millions of them and they scared everybody. They loved martial arts and weapons and they wandered around in packs and you got out of their way. Their pharmaceuticals of choice were speed and crystal meth. Not exactly fun drugs.

But then there were the Funnies, the opposite of all that, the fans of Omega the rock star, the blue-painted bad boy who danced and sang, Omega the Cajun, the master of mischief. The Funnies were the jokers, the goofballs, the clowns, the party animals. the stoners, the lovers of the wild side of rock n roll. They painted themselves blue, wore white wigs, smoked weed and spent their time listening to Omega's great sexy music and laughing a lot.

It depended entirely on your temperament which one you were, a Finnie or a Funnie. But between them they had pop culture sewn up tighter than a camel's ass in a sandstorm, and both were 100% Omega. On hallowe'en, children on one side of the street dressed as Finnie zombies and vampires. Across the street the Funnie kids had bright blue body suits and blue-painted faces, wore white wigs and giggled a lot.

It was Style Wars, and both sides were Omega, making the Cajuns filthy, crazy, stinkin' rich.

The Finnies were the dark side, the Funnies the wacky side of Omega. At the Macy's Day parade, it was a big blue jolly Omega Finn that floated down Broadway, not a scary black Finnie. And then there was Brazil.

Twenty Seven

Ah, yes. Brazil.

You would think that Brazil couldn't get any crazier, but it did.

Brazil got hit by a double whammy. Omega Finn *and* Macumba. In Brazil, Macumba was just as big as Omega. She was their new star, their latest claim to fame, the world's biggest supermodel from a country that cranks them out like samba tunes. She was all that and rumored to be a juju princess too. Pure jungle. Not just Brazilian. *Amazonian,* baby. And in a world where black and white races have mixed to create such cute people, she was both and neither. She was some spectacular kind of rare albino. Pale gold skin, gold hair, golden eyes and that golden smile. She was pure gold. She was unique.

And Omega's music was just the right style for the sexy samba and the voodoo vibe. And the blue paint and white wig? Heaven sent.

Nudity is already pretty much mandatory on Brazil beaches, where topless women wear only a piece of string in their ass crack. At Carnival, who has time for a piece of string? The clubs are like nudist camps.

With Macumba's reputation for walking around naked, and Omega's blue body paint hitting the scene at the same time, that was all the excuse a woman needed to go *totally* naked in public. This is, lest we forget, the home of the Brazilian Wax. And if a totally naked girl is covered in blue paint, well, she isn't *entirely* nude, is she?

So, there were several samba schools at the Carnival parade in the Samba-Drome all done up in a blue Omega theme, blue paint, white wigs, and nothing else. Totally naked. Officially, it was a scandal, but privately? Everybody loved it. Ministers and CEOs proudly paraded their wives and daughters around at the chicest parties in only paint and a wig and they were not just respectable, they were well dressed.

At Carnival, Omega's band were the stars wherever they went. juju jokers. Far from the dour, black-clad Finnies at home in the US. They were fun. They rocked. Omega Finn himself was elusive and never seen, as per legend, but the band were non-stop out and about, having the time of their lives, often accompanied by this guy Oliver. Who was he? Omega's right hand man? Who knew? Who cared? He was cute. He was fun. It was all fun. Fun 'n' games. Rock 'n' roll

Twenty Eight

Any other bunch of lunatics might have had their heads turned by all that money. But not Oliver's band. Not The Fear.

They could have turned into real assholes, the way many rock n roll musicians do when luck fills their pockets with diamonds and makes them think they deserve it. Not these guys. They were dyed in the wool Cajun rockers and, as far as they were concerned, that was already the greatest accolade on earth, that alone made them special and had done so from the start when they didn't have ten cents to scratch their teenage asses with. They had always just dug who they were. They were themselves. And getting suddenly richer than shit just made them themselves but a little more so.

They had style. They always did have style. They knew what they liked. They had always dressed in a certain punky way, getting their girlfriends to sew up their own wacky designs. So they continued to do that. Fancy labels didn't do it for them. They were beyond that.

They dug old Chevvies, Fords and Caddies and customized them by hand, cutting and hammering and welding all night over a six-pack or two, and that's what they still did now, instead of strolling into a Ferrari showroom and dropping a million bucks on somebody else's idea of a cool car. Where was the fun in that?

As for behavior? Well, they had a perfect record of eventually being kicked out of every joint they frequented, and now that they were so famous, maybe they got kicked out a bit more gently and were asked for autographs as they hit the sidewalk. But that's about it. When you have a carefully refined 'modus operandi', why screw with it? That was basically their motto. And they stuck with it.

In the 60s, a famous rhinestone cowboy named Nudie had customized a big Cadillac with a huge pair of Texas cattle horns sticking out of the hood threatening to castrate any guy who came too close. The boys saw that in a book and copied it. When they needed to show up together, or just for the hell of it, they would pile into their horned Caddy, crank up the music and scare the shit out of everybody. Cops just loved pulling them over in that evil looking thing, the Fearmobile, mostly just to get a selfie.

When the Omega Finn operation moved to New York from LA, The band drove across country together in the Fearmobile towing a classic Airstream trailer full of girls, and bought the Flatiron Building, one of Manhattan's most distinguished old skyscrapers right on the corner of Madison Square and Broadway, shaped like a wedge of cheese, a building so iconic every visitor to New York has photographed it. They bought it for cash.

They had the roof covered with real grass and had a big military helicopter place four big Airstream trailers on it, one for each guy, although Oliver lived mainly elsewhere, being too busy with the non-stop slog that kept the creative output bubbling forth.

The four big, shiny futuristic aluminum pods were arranged around a plastic inflatable kiddie pool with pink plastic palm trees. The guys moved in. Several girls moved in, too. It was like a shiny little village. With dogs. And chickens. Swamp chic. Totally out of place. Anything for a laugh - one of the laughs being target practice at the occasional drone that a fan or a reporter dared to send up, to catch a glimpse of this outrageous lifestyle. Splat! So long, sucker.

They left the rest of the entire building empty except for the ground floor which they turned into a workshop for their cars. Squatters moved into the lower floors and they let them. It got to be known as The Fear Building, always surrounded by armed cops. There goes the neighborhood. Oh, well. And it had been one of the fanciest and most expensive neighborhoods on Earth. Oops!

The 'elsewhere' that Oliver lived in, quietly and in total secrecy, was in Brooklyn, in that stretch of snooty old-money townhouses called Brooklyn Heights, high above the East River, with the world famous view of downtown Manhattan beloved of movie directors and the printers of postcards. Unbeknownst to his filthy rich neighbors, he owned three of the most desirable of the houses, situated next door to each other, that a developer had knocked together while retaining the outside appearance of three separate residences.

It had a walled garden surrounding a small lawn, with ivy covering the high stone wall to keep out prying eyes. But there were no prying eyes, because nobody had any idea who the quiet young gentleman in residence was. And he took care to keep it that way.

Twenty Nine

Macumba finally met Oliver at an Omega Finn concert.

Well, they called them concerts for want of a better word, and words fail everyone who has tried to describe them, including me, and I was there that night and had total access all over the show, and still can barely believe what I saw. And what I saw was just another night, just one more wild ride on the Omega Finn worldwide runaway express train, off the rails and on fire.

An Omega Finn 'concert' was somewhere between a circus, a horror movie, a religious revival, an acid trip, a black mass, a public hanging, an orgy, a coronation, a mass hallucination, a Nazi Rally and... a rock concert.

And it was also an awe-inspiring and magical spectacle.

This one was planned to be doubly spectacular because it was in New York, across the Hudson River in Giants Stadium, a huge 70s high-sided bowl, built to hold 80,000 screaming football fans, but they were expecting far more than that, and these fans had started screaming weeks before.

Not only was I given total access, they had cameras everywhere recording everything from every angle, even unguarded talk, and I was given all of it, so you know I'm not making this shit up.

Macumba was a special guest and was flying in from some big fashion shoot on the West Coast. Macumba never said much in public, her English still not all that great, but it was known that she had a low opinion of Omega Finn and his supposed magic powers.

She had grown up among real voodoo, women who could kill with a word, men who could paralyze you. So she knew that this big Omega Finn cult was bullshit, a showman getting rich and having fun by scaring suckers who knew nothing of the real thing.

She had already felt the real thing stir in her, just like the village women said she would. She shrugged it off, wanting nothing to do with it. But she was starting to admit that it was there, scarily, inside her. But Omega Finn? She could see right through him. All bullshit. But he was very cute. And he was funny. And sexy...and...

...and then she got a shock. A big one. The moment her flight hit the ground at New York's La Guardia Airport, she got a taste of the power, the incredible juice, of the Omega Finn phenomenon.

Two red helicopters were blocking the runway.

The big Boeing was forced to stop dead. Luggage burst out of the overhead bins. People screamed. Everybody yelled at once. The Captain ran out of the cockpit into First Class where Macumba was in the front row and started yelling. Cabin staff ran over to the main door, saying that somebody was banging on it from outside.

The Captain freaked, barking at the cabin crew *not* to open it.

- But he's got a gun!

- What? Oh, here, let me... Jesus, he's got a gun!

- Open the fucking door!

- OK. OK. Opening the door!

The door opens. A rush of air into First Class. Two tall guys stride in, dressed head to foot in red skin-tight leather with red helmets and red mirror visors, waving assault rifles and yelling for everybody to step back. Everybody steps back, scared shitless.

The captain, livid at an outrage that breaks all aviation law, steps forward and yells at one of the red guys. A mistake. The guy flips up his mirrored red visor. Underneath are two glowing lenses over his eyes. A stab of laser shoots from them and knocks the captain back and he rubs a spot on his forehead as if he's been burned.

The other red ninja leans down to Macumba and gestures to her, gently, to take his hand and to get up. She takes it. She gets up. She's in a daze. She's nearly wetting herself. He speaks soothingly.

- Please relax, Miss Macumba. Omega Finn sends his regards.

- Whu?

- Please come with us now. Your luggage is taken care of.

Outside, high in the air, clinging to the two red guys, she's lowered on a fire-engine ladder to the ground, terrified. Each guy takes a hand and she walks like a little girl between them to the two red choppers, their rotors thundering overhead. She is helped aboard one of them.

They take off in formation. She sits between the two guys, shaking.

- Wh...where are we going, please?

- To the concert.

Thirty

Inside Giants Stadium it's a scene out of Dante's *Inferno.*

Screaming Hell. Deafening Hell. Medieval Hell. Punk Hell. Hell on acid. A cast of thousands of roaring, fighting, screaming, foot-stomping, flag-waving, punching, hollering, murderous Finnie lunatics packed from floor to rafters all around this big bowl, a hellish circle of cranked-up, drugged-up, amped-up whipped-up howling horror.

Behold the Finnies. Eighty thousand of them and there's another sea of them outside fighting to get in, plus millions around the world on satellite. These are the fuel that stokes the machine, the Fucking Finnies, as they refer to themselves, or just the FFs for short.

If you want to judge an artist by his fans, you would have a pretty low opinion of Omega Finn's art. But if you want to judge a charismatic leader by his apostles, well, you would have to admit, this sonofabitch must have some hellacious power to summon a seething global ocean of blind faith like the Finnies.

The Finnies are a force of nature, a multi-million strong army of mindless, brainless Omega Finn worshipers. By the time the concerts were up and running, The Fear was so much a part of everyday life for a large part of the world population that even if you didn't really believe that Omega Finn had the power to destroy anything he turned his hand to, you would still keep a few of those CDs of *The End* about you and in your car for fear of upsetting somebody who *did* believe and was afraid to be with you because you *didn't.* It was a cult of fear that had invaded life and there was no way of avoiding it, except among groups of Funnies who could laugh at it all in the privacy of their own homes.

But the Finnies were just slaves to it. Totally convinced. Utterly lost in belief, like those medieval Christians. Scared of even daring to think that Omega was not all-powerful and must be shown loyalty in public. They showed this by their outfits. The Finnies looked, collectively and individually, just astonishing.

And at an Omega Finn concert, they all came out to flash their wild outfits as proof of how crazy they were about their guru.

They were a sight, a raging madhouse of crazed outfits, all of them black, a jumble of spike-haired hardcore punks, druids in robes, bikers in leather, pirates, clowns, military freaks, all in black with the white Pentagraph sewn onto their clothes or painted or tattooed onto their skin, a black-clad circus of lunatics showing off to each other in a kind of competitive madness.

Camera crews would move around the running tracks, taking shots of this black sea of Finnies, stoned stupid, cranked on speed, fighting and dancing in flowing robes, medieval capes, ripped teeshirts, mohawks, leather, rubber, top-hats, witches' hats, devils' horns, sharkskin suits, bare-breasted women with white painted Pentagraphs on their black-painted skin, a roaring, writhing black mass, a carnival of screaming weirdness like some zoo let loose.

Smoke bombs, distress flares, fireworks, missiles of every kind fly in all directions. Gigantic black flags wave all through the packed crowd, bearing the Pentagraph logo and the omnipresent sayings: OMEGA IS THE END, and THE END IS COMING, etc.. All the same gigantic size, all printed in the same font, all official flags of this global movement all waving to the beat of ground-buzzing Omega Finn tracks, sexy, funky, slithery slinky shit, blasting out of speaker towers the size of up-ended trucks.

And that was just the crowd.

More shocking still were the armed forces sent out to control them, the notorious RedEyes.

It was two RedEyes that were sent to stop the big jet airliner on the runway and extract Macumba. Just two. And at the concerts there was an army of them. At the New York concert they stood in a ring around the running track, facing the screaming crowd, just willing them to try to get past them, so they could knock them down, beat them, and chuck them back into the crowd every few minutes. They were supposed to be Security, but they were sadistic martial arts thugs showing off to each other. Katsu, the killer Head of Security encouraged brutality and hired them for their ferocity. And the Finnies seemed to be proud of them in some sick way, boasting of times they got beaten by a RedEye, proudly showing their bruises and scars.

Picture it. A ring of tall red leather ninjas in red helmets with red mirrored visors, holding short clubs at the ready, tasers in holsters on their hips like gunfighters ready to shoot, staring down a bank of roaring fans all around the big bowl of Giants Stadium. Others are on horseback like knights with samurai helmets and bullwhips, all in red, their horses clad in red armor with red blinders and faceplates with a red horn like an ironic unicorn, there to run down any fool who dares get past the line of RedEyes. They catch them in a few strides and cut them down with their whips.

A deafening red chopper hovers to pick up the badly hurt and whisk them up and away to a field hospital in back, to get patched up and sent home after signing a release, in order to spare The Final Corporation lawsuits for actual manslaughter.

Does this sound like a rock concert to you? Me neither.

It didn't feel like one to Oliver or Leo or Madame Joy either. But they couldn't stop it now. They had created something that had gotten way out of hand. But there were no brakes on the roller coaster. At some point it had become mandatory for the crowd to get cranked up on speed and crystal meth, so what started out as pleasantly stoned rock n roll concerts got violent fast. Crowds split into gangs that would fight each other in the stands like soccer hooligans, before the show began, and that was all the excuse Katsu needed to deploy his killer RedEyes to keep them off the field and in the stands, by any means necessary, the more brutal the merrier.

Omega Finn's taunting of his followers by the constant threats of bad luck and the general atmosphere of disaster created by The Fear all added to the rampant head of steam building up to showtime, so that every few minutes, a crazed Finny would burst out onto the track to make it onto the field for no good reason other than to have a RedEye or two club him down like a dog with sickening blows from a cosh or a taser and toss him back, bloody and dazed, and give each other a high five. Masochistic madness. All part of the buzz. By the time the show started, nerves were so ragged and the raw violence so barely contained, that even the TV announcers, kept in a big cage for their own protection, feared for their lives.

Thirty One

The two red choppers bringing Macumba from her abduction at the airport, roar over the rim, into the bowl. One of them lands on top of the control booth, a long black glass box, built for the event halfway up one side of the stadium and surrounded by the screaming crowd. Waiting to meet her on the glass roof is Katsu, dressed like his troops, but with a red crest on top of his helmet like some mad psychedelic red centurian, show-off that he is.

Macumba, tiny and frail in the green hooded robe she wore for the flight, is helped down from the chopper and handed over to Katsu who escorts her down steps into the big glass booth.

Inside is another world entirely. A silent, dark cave of calm, all quiet professional activity. Leo's people. The loud, pounding music outside is muted to a soft beat that you can feel more than hear. The long dark room is on two levels, the top one set back, a bank of leather swivel chairs with butlers fussing over the Gang of Four and a few guests. Mona's two dobermans lie at her feet.

The lower level is a sea of screens and read-outs, with techies in contrast to everyone else with their sloppy teeshirts and baseball caps, thirty of them, all races, all sexes, all nerdy, staring into screens, oblivious to everything else. In the context of the barely contained hysteria on the other side of the glass, it's so smooth and casual that it's shocking. Relaxed efficiency. Screens all flashing graphics, geometrics, code. In this dark world the screens are like hedgerows of bright blossoms. The shiny red figure of Katsu strides through it, trailing Macumba, her head on a swivel. RedEyes here and there check the countdown on screens as Katsu nods to them. 15:31. 15:30. 15:29.

Fifteen minutes to showtime.

He removes his helmet and tosses it to a RedEye as he reaches Main Control where Leo sits cross-legged like a Buddha, elevated in a high swivel armchair, overlooking a semi-circle of monitors three or four deep, each with a different image, ahead of him a complete panoramic view of the playing field. And it's empty.

Mere minutes before showtime and there's nothing. No stage. Nothing. Just an empty green field. 14:57. 14:56. 14:55.

Outside in the stadium, everything slowly changes.

The pounding, slinky, sexy music fades. All the lights dim. The yelling stops. A deep rumbled murmur takes over, as the crowd anticipates the start of the show. All the red choppers lift off and disappear over the rim of the bowl. The mounted troops trot off the field. The RedEyes facing the mob, all take a knee. It's quiet. Eerie. Just the sound of the TV commentators in their big cage yammering away in the distance trying to describe all this to live audiences around the world. There's nothing on the grass field. The commentators can't believe that with minutes to go, there's still nothing there. Countdown shows on all screens: 7:46, 7:45, 7:44...

Inside the black glass room at Main Control, Leo appears relaxed. Mid-20s, handsome, prematurely grey hair shoulder-length, neatly combed, Hawaiian shirt, cross-legged, barefoot, staring at the screens in his high chair, hitting buttons with one hand, Coke can in the other, speaking quietly to a female voice on the intercom, with the whole sequence recorded for review.

- Holograms nine through forty all set?
- At your mark, Leo. One min twenty secs
- Effects forty thru eighty-two standby?
- At your mark, Leo. One min ten secs.

Katsu arrives with Macumba and Leo glances at them.

- OK outside, Katsu?
- All OK.
- Cops cool?
- Cops staying out of it.
- That's what Oliver pays 'em to do.

Katsu leaves with Macumba, escorting her upstairs to join the VIPs She is seated next to Mona Callan who, clearly jealous, makes a big show of ignoring her, while Steiner all but drools over her and Di Stefano kisses her hand fawningly. The dogs sniff her feet.

Down at Main Control, the clock is running down to zero.

- All effects armed?
- All armed. Leo. At your mark.
- Thank you, Baby. Lights out?
- Blackout ready. At ten, nine, eight, seven....

Blackout. Total sudden blackness outside. At that same instant, a big power chord blasts out and shakes the stadium and a ring of huge klieg lights shoot straight up in a circle all the way around the rim of the great bowl, visible from space. Screams from the fans.

Then cheers and gasps, as they look up and see, caught in the circle of vertical lights, a big red pyramid floating in the black sky above the stadium, slowly turning and gently falling into the stadium, as the loud power chord rings out and turns into a jingling, throbbing jungle sound of birds and whistling wind. The huge red pyramid descends slow and stately into the bowl and gently settles in the center of the green playing field.

Inside the glass box, Macumba is on the edge of her seat just amazed at the sight of the gigantic pyramid that is not really there, falling into the stadium. She grins at Mona Callan, who affects boredom and sips her martini, wearing small chic ear phones. At her feet, her two dogs sit up and growl. Macumba is handed earphones to get the full effect of what's going on outside.

Outside, the low rumble of the jungle sounds gets louder and more rhythmic as the red pyramid starts to pulsate with inner light, throbbing in time to the beat which is getting so loud that many in the crowd put hands to ears until... Boom!...a flash of white light blinds everyone momentarily as the klieg lights turn off. The beat becomes part of an Omega Finn song that all the Finnies know, and a cheer goes up as they all start swaying to it, and look up.

As eyes adjust after the big flash, the sky is transformed into a galaxy of stars and beautiful planets of different colors that whirl and turn over the stadium as comets whizz across the sky, all to the irresistable beat, in a pure, psychedelic fantasy.

It's an extraordinarily beautiful sight, a total mood shift from the raucous, violent mayhem of a few minutes earlier. The crowd is entranced into silence by the sight, swaying to the soulful jungle rhythm as they look up at the planetary light show in the sky and the red pyramid glowing and throbbing to the beat.

Such sweetness and light. Such peace and love and psychedelia. Really? Where are we? Is this the 60s, or an Omega Finn concert?

Or is the guy just setting everybody up for a kick in the ass?

Thirty Two

In Brooklyn Heights, in the cavernous hanger-like basement of Oliver's joined-together town houses, as the millions of windows in all the skyscrapers of Lower Manhattan across the East River blaze into the night like the earth's biggest jukebox, a woman's hand in a thin latex glove is dabbing blue body paint with a small sponge onto Oliver's painted blue face, applying a few finishing touches.

His whole body in its skintight sheath is bright blue, as are his hands and feet. Other gloved hands place a shiny white, shoulder length wig on his head. He checks himself in a mirrored wall, doing a few bends and squats to make sure the stretchy costume moves freely, moving his head to check the fit of the wig. He turns and walks away into the center of the giant space. Its walls, ceiling and floor are all painted a seamless, solid bright green.

Now he's Omega Finn, a small blue and white figure in a big green world. All round him at a short distance are banks of cameras, lasers, mirrors, cables and all the other paraphernalia of Leo's holography, out there on the wingtip of the science of which he is master and magician.

All over Oliver's body and head are tiny colored dots that map the contours of his limbs for the benefit of the motion-capture cameras that will trace his every movement and transform them into the holographic 3D Omega Finn in Giant's Stadium.

In front of Oliver is a bank of screens showing the stadium from various angles, with its overhead planetary show and red pyramid pulsating, with sound turned down low, so he can hear Leo through his earphones, and make the moves they've rehearsed.

The fans at his concerts know that the Omega Finn performing for them is a hologram. But they also know that somewhere, the 'real' Omega is doing it all live, with his band. And sure enough, the band is set up just a few feet away, all staring at their own screens, playing live. It's a point of pride for them and for Oliver that this is live. This is a real band. A working band. This is core Rock 'n' roll.

- Mickey Mouse 53. Ready?
- At your mark, Leo. Mickey Mouse.
- OK, baby. Hit it!

Thirty Three

Over the rim of the stadium, two gigantic white three-fingered cartoon gloves, like Mickey Mouse's hands, rise into the sky full of stars and planets, one at each end of the big bowl, disembodied, each as big as an apartment building, but rising with effortless fluidity, clicking their fingers to the beat. Mind-blowing.

Even the RedEyes on the running track, turn and look up, the colossal white hands reflected in their red mirror visors. The crowd all cheer and laugh, mimicking these huge gloved cartoon hands, holding their own hands high in the air and clicking their fingers in time with them, to the rhythm of the slinky, sexy music.

Inside the glass box, Macumba is wide-eyed, hands over mouth with surprise and shock and delight. The dogs, on their feet, growl.

The white gloves wrap their fingers over the rim, one at each end, like fingers gripping a serving bowl, as the big red pyramid still throbs to the beat. There are shrieks of delight as the big hands slowly seem to spin the stadium clockwise. The sky full of stars is actually spinning slowly counter-clockwise and the red pyramid is spinning with it in the same direction, but it feels as if they're standing still and the stadium itself is moving. The illusion is that the entire stadium is being spun slowly on its axis by two big white cartoon hands, with the stars and the pyramid staying in place. It's a superb effect, so real and believable that some in the stands hold on to each other and almost lose their balance as the stadium feels like it's slowly turning in space.

There are astonished, delighted reactions all through the crowd and a wave of applause and chants of Omega! Omega! Omega!. This is all so new. Nobody has ever seen or imagined such wonder. It's holographic illusion on such a huge scale that it's barely possible. And if the show were to end there, everybody would still be talking about it for years, in terms of pure amazement and delight.

They have no idea what is about to happen.

Slowly, a sound of laughter mixes with the music, which starts to fade out, until loud laughter is all that's left, echoing around the stands. Then the laughter turns ugly. Demonic. Evil. Fiendish. And the spinning starts to speed up. Faster and faster, the white hands whip the stadium around at a quickening, sickening clip. The crowd screams. Many lose their balance and fall over, some of the RedEyes, too. It's now a wildly spinning bowl, out of control in this strange universe, at the mercy of the two hands. A loud whistling-wind sound-effect adds to the awful sense of spinning. People are on their knees or lying on the floor, nauseated, all screaming, begging for this to stop. But it doesn't. It gets faster, and faster and the evil, lunatic laughter gets louder and louder. Above, the pretty planets become a blur of gory, horrifying colors, blood reds and purples, the red pyramid pulsing brighter and brighter, faster and faster. The crowd is caught in a horrifying mass torture, crying, begging for this cruel game to stop.

Then, mercifully, it does. The hands let go of the rim and open up their palms to show that they are done with their naughty game. The stadium appears to slow down and gently come to a stop. The ugly, scary colors above all disappear, leaving only a clear night sky. It takes a few minutes for the crowd to resume its former balance and for those on the floor to get up and calm down. In the interim, the cool, slinky music has resumed and very quickly everything is back to the former great mood, with the whole crowd chattering and laughing about the brief and brilliant scare their own adored guru has just put into them. Bravo! Good for him! What a genius! Typical Omega Finn! He really got us that time!

With the good mood now restored, the big hands slowly sail towards each other, meet high over the pyramid, and start clapping to the beat and finger-popping to the off-beat. The audience cheers and imitates them once again. They and the crowd are now one big happy rhythm box. Now that every pair of hands in the crowd is clapping and finger popping, the two big hands start to play. They lower themselves into the stadium and pass over each other like the hands of an old-school magician about to do a trick.

One of the hands delicately picks up the pyramid, turns it over, placing it on its point, into the upturned palm of the other hand, then does a little wrist motion and points to it as if to say Ta- da!

A huge cheer from the crowd, all now frankly spellbound. The hand puts its middle finger to its thumb, as if to flick something, then approaches the edge of the pyramid, and with a neat flick, sets it spinning slowly on its tip on the other hand's upturned palm. More cheers.

The other hand, the one with the red pyramid now spinning in its palm, tosses the spinning pyramid in the air. It lands, still spinning, on the raised fingertip of the other hand, like a basketball player spinning a ball. It's now the turn of the other hand to do the 'Ta-Dah!' An even bigger cheer echoes around the stadium. This is such colossal holography that none of the TV reporters can believe it any more than the thousands of stoned Finnies, and it all just goes on, amazing move after move. And all this is just the prelude.

The fingertip with the spinning pyramid tosses it up in the air and it falls to earth, planting itself on its point into the green playing field with a dramatic thud! on the sound system, and that stops the music dead. There's dead silence, just the low murmur of a huge crowd stunned into silence and wondering what can possibly come next. The red pyramid is now upside down, its point stuck in the ground and its upturned flat base now perfectly parallel to the playing field.

Murmurs go around the crowd. Could the upturned base of this pyramid be the stage that Omega will appear on? They have seen Omega Finn appear as a hologram in all kinds of situations before, and everyone knows that when this happens it is as much for his own safety as for the spectacle, but that he is performing live, at a safe distance, his hologram merely following his actual live moves. But there is no time for speculation. It's all moving too fast.

There is a loud drumroll, the kind of cheap, cheesy sound you hear in a circus, announcing 'here comes the big trick!' - a touch of pure irony for something so state-of-the-art and amazing. And just like a cheap magician, one hand makes a fist and turns itself over, as the other hand points to it. The drumroll continues. The fingers slowly open to reveal what it is holding. In its splayed open palm is the small figure of a man. It's Omega Finn.

The place goes nuts. Wild cheering and chants of Omega! Omega! as he stands there, raising his arms slowly to the crowd.

Thirty Four

In the Brooklyn basement, Oliver raises his arms slowly to the crowd, receiving the adulation that he can only see on the screens in front of him as he turns this way and that, to acknowledge the whole massive crowd, while listening to Leo continue in his relaxed drawl to his female producer.

- OK. Blue Boy looking good. Effect 89?

- 89 set, Leo. At your mark.

- OK. 89. Blue Boy. Finger walk. Hit it!

Oliver mimes taking a few steps forward.

In the stadium, Omega Finn steps forward from the palm of the big white glove and dances along its extended forefinger, as the hand moves over to touch the red pyramid, and he alights from the finger onto the pyramid and struts across it, singing...

'I ain't givin' you the finger.
I ain't givin' you a hand.
I'm just minding my own
And owning your mind...'

In the Brooklyn basement and in Giants Stadium, Oliver and Omega move together in sync, one by a green screen, the other on a red pyramid that isn't there. And the band plays on, live and loud, a few feet from Oliver, their eyes on him for cues.

The two colossal hands rise up slowly to the rim of the stadium, clicking their fingers to the rhythm of the music and they slowly disappear over the edge, waving to the crowd as they do, and as Omega turns and waves goodbye to them, the crowd all wave together a fond farewell to the hands that so recently spun them around in terror, all forgiven in this mass musical love-in.

And so Omega kicks off the concert, running through a bunch of his multi-million-seller songs of sinuous, swampy, sexy, funky, bluesy rock, all reinforcing the ideas of luck, and fate and control of your destiny and doing the right thing, an ambiguous, sadistic but sexy rabble-rousing feel of being together for a purpose but without saying what that purpose is.

It's a brilliant balancing act, all wrapped up in sex and swagger, leaving the entire audience feeling part of something powerful but unstated, involving but indescribable. It's the essence of religious fervor without the religion, the lyrics projecting a man with immense power that he can't believe, and doesn't want, but can't escape from, doomed to fame and influence and yet somehow lost and helpless, Omega dancing along a tightrope of pure suggestion and innuendo, eliciting love, admiration, brotherhood and even pity for the trap he finds himself in as the helpless vessel of prophesy, unable to turn off the tap of prediction and knowledge, all this seductive manipulation belying the overriding fact that the entire crowd and everyone watching around the world, entranced and seduced, is actually terrified of him. But for the moment they have forgotten The Fear, the thing that has brought them here into his grip.

Right now, the spectacle is too overwhelming. Omega is dancing around on an upturned red glowing pyramid as he runs through these vaguely disturbing but kick-ass rock songs. And the sights just keep coming, one after the other.

Four more huge red pyramids slowly sprout from the playing field, rising up into the air, almost filling the stadium, flipping slowly upside down like the one that he is dancing on, then slowly rotating around the center one, and now Omega is skipping from one to another, dancing and singing his well-known lyrics, the band in Brooklyn belting out their great live sound, keeping it all rocking.

And then suddenly there are multiple Omegas, one on each stage, then two on each stage, then ten on each, all moving in sync and the crowd howling with amazement as the band hits one last big power chord that echoes around the bowl and the fifty Omegas all stand still, feet apart, arms out, taking in the waves of applause as the four new pyramids rise up into the air, ten Omegas on each, up and up, disappearing into the black night sky, leaving one pyramid with its ten Omegas. Then nine of the remaining ones evaporate in a shower of colorful pixels, leaving only the one Omega standing there.

Slowly he falls to his hands and knees as if worn out, the crowd roaring, whistling and stamping for more. But there is no more.

A deep bass chord swells. The crowd is bathed in deep blue light. They quieten down. They know what's about to happen.

Thirty Five

In the VIP section of the glass box, Macumba looks around nervously, wondering why this silence and this eerie dark blue light have replaced the fun and the dancing and the fabulous music. The dobermans whimper and go to hide behind Mona's chair.

In Central Control, Leo yawns, stretches and asks for a new Coke, then sits back down and focuses again at the screens in front of him, talking quietly to his producer.

In the Brooklyn basement, the band wipe away sweat, tune their guitars and stand ready, looking at Oliver, awaiting his signal.

Oliver, still on his hands and knees, not moving, is preparing for his big moment.

In the stadium, Omega is on his hands and knees and still not moving, bathed in the eery dark blue light. The crowd is quiet. They're murmuring to each other. They seem afraid. They have been here before.

The RedEyes, who were taking a knee during the singing and dancing, have stood up again, facing the crowd, braced for action.

The TV reporters in their big cage talk quietly in their many languages, trying to convey the sense of forboding, the unease that has suddenly overtaken the stadium. Those who have attended other concerts are staring at the red pyramid and at Omega down on all fours, head bowed. They know what is about to come. They know he's not exhausted. He's an animal ready to pounce.

As he remains there, down on all fours, a dark rumble starts to echo around the stands bathed in this scary blue light, a deep rumbling like the growl of a giant predator, a hypnotic growl that in the forest would stop prey dead in its tracks, terrified.

Above, there's a sudden loud screech like metal scraping on stone, as five massive steel bars grow out from opposite sides of the big bowl and meet in the middle with a loud clunk, the symbolism is unmistakable. This is jail. You're trapped. Nobody gets out of here unscathed. As if the ring of brutal sadists in red leather has left that in any doubt.

Omega Finn slowly raises his head while staying down on his

hands and knees, staring into the stands, giving an even stronger impression of an animal picking out its prey, its victim, its next kill.

He moves his head around slowly and stops. He holds his stare.

In the section of the crowd he appears to be looking at, there is a sudden commotion. People look around at each other, hurriedly, anxiously. Couples hold on to each other, those outside the focus of Omega's gaze, pull away, trying to separate themselves.

From the rim of the stadium behind Omega, from up among those gigantic prison bars, several laser beams shoot out and all converge precisely on that same bunch of Finnies and light them up brightly, pitilessly. They scream. They cover their eyes. They get down on their knees. They look out helplessly at the red pyramid and at Omega, their tormentor. He speaks. It's an awful sound.

It's a deep whisper that's loud enough to reverberate around the whole stadium, a rough rasping whisper that he projects through the sound system, perfectly audible everywhere in the huge bowl, as he channels a very old man's voice that is not his own, as if he's in the grip of a voodoo spirit, but not flailing and lost as if possessed. This is calm and controlled, focused and sharp, aimed like a dagger at the writhing, helpless group of Finnies on their knees, now abandoned by all those near them, who back off and leave them like a little island of brightly lit terror.

"Who arrrre you? Who arrrrrre yoooou?", he whispers. He stands up, still staring and now pointing at the same spot.

"I know. who you are. I know. I know you. And you know that I know that you know that I know who you are, don't you? Don't you?"

There's a pause. A second's pause that's an eternity for the little brightly lit huddle of Finnies scared out of their wits.

"You know. Don't you? Don't you....*Daniel?!*

There's a yelp from someone in the little group and a pushing and shoving as they separate and scatter to all sides, leaving one young man alone in the searing spotlights, alone on his knees in a kind of helpless supplication, helpless and hopeless as in turns out.

"That's right, Danny boy,' says Omega in his scary raspy voice, moving to the edge and pointing at the pariah that the crowd is now shunning in a wide arc, struggling to get away from him.

"C'mon down, baby," says Omega, pointing. "C'mon down, and get saved, you misguided, misbegotten little maggot."

Scattered smatterings of nervous laughter sputter from the rest of the mob, relieved that they are not the ones being picked on, and that Omega has spared them his ritual public torture this time around. Other Finnies pick the guy up from his knees and help to manhandle him down the many steps to the running track where several Red Eyes grab him as roughly as possible, giving him a couple of good kicks before dragging him across the playing field and throwing him to the ground under the huge red pyramid, the pitiless spotlights following him to where he looks up helplessly at Omega towering over him. Omega meanwhile has sat down with his legs dangling over the edge of his stage, luminous, magnificent, with his bright blue body and long silvery hair against the bright glowing red of the upturned pyramid and the weird blue darkness that dims the whole stadium.

He looks down at his crumpled victim, while swinging his legs in the most casual, playful boyish manner.

"Well, hey now. Lookee here, ladies and germs. Danny boy. Dan the Man. A dude with a 'tude. A little dude with a big mouth"

Omega gets back to his feet and walks around the stage, talking to his fans, his eery old-man voice gone, now just his normal cocky self. Below him, the RedEyes surround their victim ominously.

"Not so big now, are we, big boy, not so proud, not so loud, eh? This little pebble in my shoe, this loudmouth has the nerve to doubt my powers of prophesy, prediction, divination, of getting inside your head. Never question that, boys and girls. This bigshot here tried very hard to hide his aliases, his avatars, his doppelgangers. But not from me, boys and girls. No. That is simply impossible.

"So how did I find this spreader of lies? With an army of hackers? With a webful of spiders? No. I don't need any of those."

He sits down crosslegged in the center of the upturned pyramid. The pyramid starts to rotate very slowly, sweeping his gaze around the crowd as he chats away, quietly, calmly, relaxed.

"So, how do I do it? I do nothing. I empty my brain. I lay down in the moonlight. Alone. I swim in the starlight. All alone. And the fish just simply swims to me. Just like that. I don't fish. I catch.

"I saw the lies he was telling as I lay in the moonlight. I slid into his mind. And here he is now. Look at him. You wanna wind up like him? I don't fish. I catch. I slip into your mind. Mental burglary.

"And you're next. That's right. If you spread the same lie that this fool tried to spread, the lie that Omega Finn is a fake, then you're next. If you're even *dreaming* that, you better wake up and apologize."

He stands up. He claps his hands. The dimmed lights fade up.

The red pyramid still spins slowly. He spreads his arms and smiles.

"So! Tell me! what shall I do with him? Shall my boys beat the shit out of him?" A huge cheer goes up. "Nah. Not this time. Fear is the key. Daniel has now known The Fear. The truth will follow."

He stands on the edge of the pyramid looking down.

"Let him go, my fearsome RedEye brethren. He's served his pathetic purpose. The little ones... we throw back."

The RedEyes drag him up, march him across grass and hurl him back into the crowd, no doubt to be beaten much worse by them.

"Here endeth the lesson!" Omega yells at them on his rotating platform. He's now animated, stalking around his stage, as the music starts to swell and the lights get brighter.

"See those steel bars up there above me? They are my prison. Not yours, baby. Mine. It is I who am imprisoned. Not you."

The five huge prison bars start to glow bright white, detach from the rim and float slowly down into the stadium, turning over until they stand on end above the pyramid like a huge ladder up to the sky.

A roar rises from the crowd. The five bars are now the Pentagraph!

Omega leaps up onto the first rung of the Pentagraph and swings up to the next and then the next as he yells out his big farewell.

"My power is my prison. Not yours. I don't want it. I don't like it. I don't need it. But I have it! I have the power! Pray for me!"

On the top rung, at a dizzying height, all necks craning up to watch him, he stands upright, arms spread out, raising them high, yelling "What's my name? What's my name? What's my name?"

The crowd roars back, "Omega! Omega! Omega! Omega!"

And in a blinding flash of light it's all gone. The red pyramid, the Pentagraph, Omega Finn, all of it, gone, disappeared into the night. All that's left is the music, the sexy, slithery, funky rock 'n' roll music.

Thirty Six

In the Brooklyn basement, in the big green hologram factory, the band lets out a long, tired whoop and slaps five all around, with Oliver ripping off his wig and tossing it at Skins before falling on the floor and letting out a long wolf howl of relief. Cold beers are passed around, everyone flops onto the floor and joins Oliver in a pile of laughs, groans, arms, legs and sweat. Holy hammered shit! They did it again! Four bad boys from Mama Boo have again pulled off the greatest show on earth. So what's new?

Five boys, if you include Leo, the genius, who now joins them via the bank of screens on the wall, grinning and chugging an ice-cold Tin Roof beer, flown in specially from Baton Rouge, with a big fatty burning in the other hand.

- Greetings, cajun cocksuckers! (weary cheers) I guess we done ‘er. I guess we cut ‘er. Couple of very minor fuck-ups nobody noticed. So! We're waiting! Get that blue-assed baboon into the shower and get all o' y'alls butts over here! Time to party!

In the chopper, the four are still jabbering about details of the show, Oliver toweling his wet hair, saying that seeing himself so high up on the top rung of that Pentagraph, he got vertigo and nearly fell over. More high fives. More tokes. More beers.

In the glass box, the Gang of Four are in tense consultation, Katsu riled up about something, jabbing the air in a rage, Mona not noticing that her big dogs have gone over to nuzzle around Macumba, tails tucked under, and their fearsome muzzles on her lap, sniffing her and licking her hands and making purring noises more like kittens than the murderous hellhounds they are.

The band arrives and joins the mob of happy, yammering techies gathered around Leo, all drinking champagne, passing joints and slapping five with the band and with Oliver, whom they all have gotten to know during the many rehearsals and run-throughs, not knowing that Oliver is Omega, assuming that he's just the producer. Leo and Oliver always refer to Omega in the third person. He's someone else. Somewhere else. The star. Unseen.

Skins, the drummer, notices Macumba alone, and braving Mona's devil dogs, introduces himself and escorts her over to meet Oliver and Leo and the rest of the mob. The big man-eaters follow her like lapdogs, until Mona notices that they've gone, yells a command, and they trot over to her, looking scared. She leaves the big glass room with them at heel and the three other bigwigs in tow. All four executives look seriously pissed off at something and stride out of the place as if on a mission, leaving a much more pleasant and relaxed atmosphere behind them.

Macumba, in her usual adorable way, is having a great time and enchants the whole company with her sweet disposition, excited by what she has just seen and full of star-struck questions for Leo, like asking in her innocent way if his long grey hair is a sign of genius. She mingles with the rest of the techies, accepting a joint here and there and seeming not to notice how dumbstruck they all are by her astonishing beauty.

The band get introduced to Macumba after it's explained to her that they were playing the whole show live in the same remote spot where Omega Finn was singing and dancing against a green screen. She's hip to the technology and once she unravels the nerdy slang, wins big brownie points for saying that live music is the only music. High fives all around from the band, who are all seriously smitten.

They tell her that Skins gets his name from his drum skins, but also for the fact that he often plays naked so his clothes don't get wet. She tells him she was naked until she was fourteen. Skins starts to strip off and gets dragged off, laughing and protesting, as she eggs him on, with Bucket the bass man and Jones the guitarist, all getting along with her like old pals. Chicks like musicians, it's a natural fact.

Oliver is off to one side the whole time inhaling her beauty and sweetness, her dimples popping every time she smiles, which is all the time. When they are finally introduced and she asks what he does, there's an awkward moment until Jones explains that he runs the entire show and so she shakes his hand to congratulate him. He walks away, subtly sniffing his palm for traces of her loveliness.

He notices that the Gang Of Four have split and asks after them. A RedEye says, "They're off doing what they do best."

Thirty Seven

Under Giants Stadium, the scene is anything but relaxed and enjoyable. This is the vast cavern of the Omega Finn concession stands, a realm of commerce, one of the many spigots of money that float the big boat and make everyone richer by the minute. This is hardcore cash. This is the realm of the Final Corporation, the Gang Of Four, the whip hand, the piper that must be paid. And right now there appears to be a wee piper-payment problem.

It's a cathedral of concrete under the stands, full of stalls selling hotdogs and beer, and pushing Omega Finn merch and the talisman CDs, all festooned in Omega flags with the usual mottos: The End Is Here, Mega Omega, Buy Or Die, all black, all owned by The Final Corporation and that's the delicate issue that's being sorted out right now with their usual delicacy, by RedEye thugs.

A circle of leather-clad RedEyes surrounds a knot of terrified merchants, occasionally putting in a good kick to optimize the fear level as they await the wrath of the gods bearing down on them in the form of the four livid executives, Katsu, Steiner, Di Stefano and Mona Callan, her huge dobermans snorting with anticipation. They know that this where they earn their big slabs of sirloin. This is exactly what the Gang of Four does best.

They inflict fear. Whatever contract infraction these poor saps are guilty of - skimming, selling counterfeits, whatever it is, they know they won't get sued. They'll get the shit kicked out of them. They have been shown the brutal videos of what will happen, but they thought they could get away with it. No chance.

Katsu arrives first, red leather from toe to plume. He wades right in and starts kicking. Squeals of pain. Bystanders gather. RedEyes uncurl their red bullwhips and start whaling on the cowering group. Blood spurts. The dogs smell it and growl. Mona yells 'Sick 'em!" They pounce and start biting, really biting. But they've been trained on the lifelike flesh of Japanese sex dolls, by Steiner the lawyer, trained to only puncture the skin. Enough to make victims faint. But no lawsuits. They earn their expensive Kobe beef. Mona turns and snarls at the crowd, "What the fuck are you lookin' at?!"

Thirty Eight

Outside the rarified air of the glass control booth, out there in the near-deserted stadium, the RedEyes move into what would be a huge chore for most security details, but for them is the fun part of the night, beating the living shit out of the last of the Finnies who won't, or can't, go home. It's a sadist's wet dream. License to injure and terrify without check or reproach. And they do.

Bullwhips cracking and tasers crackling, they wade in with a will, inflicting exactly as much pain and hurt as they know how to, carefully, without actually involving hospitals or lawsuits, both of which will get them fired from a job that they love more than life itself.

Around the stadium there are still many thousands gathered, trading memories of this, the greatest night of their lives, but they scatter off into the night as soon as they see the crimson tide of leather and pain headed their way.

Inside the control booth, stoned and reluctant, but pretty tired too, Leo's more privileged revelers peel out in hammered and happy dribs and drabs as his little post-show after-party winds down. Oliver leads Macumba, a bit worse for wear on finest weed and champagne, up the steps to the roof of the glass box and helps her into a bright red thundering chopper to whisk her away.

- Where are we going?
- To your palace, Princess.
- But I have a reservation...
- We cancelled it. This is nicer.

She was out cold on Oliver's shoulder before the chopper was in the air and zooming over Manhattan, and he was inhaling her, in his own personal heaven. It had been quite a night and she was the icing on the cake, the loveliest girl in the world, and he knew it.

As they flew South over downtown Manhattan, Oliver looked down with satisfaction at the skyscrapers, many of which had put out their lights but had left certain key windows brightly lit so that several of the tallest towers spelled out into the black night the two words with which he had conquered half the world.

The End.

Thirty Nine

The three Finnie girls were sure this was Omega's limo slipping out the back after the show. They had a solid tip that there would be a few decoys, but that the fifth limo from Exit 17 would be the one with Omega inside.

They dogged the limo through traffic, staying a couple of cars back. They had seen enough cop shows to know this was how you tail a perp. Excitement cranked as traffic thinned and the stretch limo finally turned off into a dark side street, then ran down a ramp to a parking garage under a commercial building.

They ditched their car and skittered down the ramp on high heels. In their wacky outfits, with big black plumes and tall spiked hairdos, they looked like some clown funeral procession, any hope of not being conspicuous shot to shit.

The Cadillac's tail lights turned off and the driver's door opened. Out of it stepped a short, slightly built guy with a peaked cap, shades, and high boots worn outside his horse-riding jodhpur pants, like one of those show-jumping dudes, an outfit of such high style it got loud whispers of approval from the girls.

The chauffeur opened the passenger door and the lights went on inside. The girls ran up to it excitedly and stood in a semi-circle around the small driver. But nobody got out. The limo was empty.

'Sorry, girls", said the driver with a raspy, high-pitched laugh. "Y'all treed the wrong raccoon." He took off his peaked cap and tossed it in, followed by his chauffeur's jacket, and shut the door. He reached up and loosened his tied-up long grey hair. It fell onto his shoulders. He removed the shades and faced them in the light, so they could get their first good look. It was an old woman. It was Madame Joy.

The stunned group watched open-mouthed as Madame reached into the trunk and put on a black leather biker jacket and a yellow helmet, climbed onto a Harley, fired it up, and burned rubber out the door and up the ramp, with a long loud laugh that echoed.

"Well, I'll be fucked," says one of the girls.

"You have been," says another.

Forty

Macumba slowly comes to the surface among a heap of ultrasoft goose-down pillows and high-thread shiny white Egyptian cotton sheets. She rolls over onto her belly and stretches and rolls onto her back, frizzy golden hair spilling all over the big soft white meringue she is afloat on. Everything smells crisp and clean and feels so soft she does not want to open her eyes from this dream.

Then she snaps awake and sits up naked in a strange bed in a strange and very big room that she has no memory of coming to. As her eyes adjust in the half light, she sees her own clothes draped carefully over an antique polished wooden contraption with what looks like a mahogany clothes hanger on the top. It makes her think of Japan and her last modeling trip there. Where is she? How did she get here? An Asian accented voice comes from the big window.

- Good morning, Miss Macumba.
- Oh... good mor....
- You slept so well we did not want to wake you.
- Where are... who are...?
- Green tea with one Madelaine cookie, is that correct?
- Oh. Yes, I... thank you... I...

The big room floods with light as the tall heavy drapes are pulled back by the pretty young Asian girl in a starched maid's outfit, who bows to Macumba Kyoto-style, and opens the big glass doors onto a garden exploding with white roses in a high hedge around a small lawn. Birds are singing. The scent of the roses wafts into the big bright room as the young Asian bows herself out the door and leaves Macumba to wake up alone in a sort of trance.

She slowly slides out of bed, rubbing sleepy eyes and placing bare feet into the deep soft white carpet, and walks naked to the tall window, a tiny porcelain cup of green tea in hand, to look out at this wall of white blossom and the lush green lawn and empty blue sky, unsure if she's in Kyoto or... Tokyo, or...

The Asian girl wafts back into the room and slides open the door to the adjoining bathroom, indicating it to Macumba, who asks,

- Please.... can you tell me where we are?
- We are in Brooklyn.

Macumba steps out of the shower, still sleepy, piecing together the previous evening's events, unsure of the last few woozy details, pats herself dry with huge fluffy towels and sniffs a few *eaux de parfum*, all of which are her favorites. Clearly someone took great care to make her feel at home. So, feeling at ease, she walks back into the big bedroom, still naked, and comes to a sudden stop.

Facing her is a little old lady in biker leathers and knee high horse-riding boots, holding two yellow crash helmets, one in each hand.

- Hi, kid. I'm Madame Joy. Oliver's grandma.

Macumba covers herself with her hands and looks around for clothes.

- Forget it. If I looked that good, I'd walk down the street naked.
- Please excuse me. This is how I grew up.
- I know. And it suits you. Wanna go for a ride?
- Like this?
- No. You'll have to wear a helmet.

They look at each other. They grin. Madame tosses her a helmet.

Roaring down the road on Madame Joy's Harley, whooping and laughing, Madame in her leathers and, behind her, Macumba wearing only a helmet, buck naked, arms tight around her new best friend, they weave in and out of the disbelieving Brooklyn traffic and zoom off at top speed out onto the Long Island Expressway before anybody can think about chasing them, the oddest couple seen on a Harley Davidson in these parts in a long time, if ever.

They leave the freeway to a few honks from stunned admirers, cross the highway, putter sedately down a few tree-lined suburban streets, go off-road at the end of one of them and come out onto a long, empty, early morning beach. They ride the length of the long, deserted sands with the morning sun glinting on the Atlantic.

- Where are we going?
- To my place.
- A beach house?
- Better. You're gonna love it.

At the end of the beach there's an old ramp once used for launching boats, and Madame rides up it, turns, and follows a path down into a tiny hidden cove. On its little beach stands a small, wooden gypsy caravan painted red, yellow and green.

"Wow," says Macumba. "I told ya", says Madame Joy.

Forty One

The Pritzker Prize is the biggest award in architecture.

Oliver won it for the HQ of The Final Corporation the year it opened, to worldwide acclaim, the building that came to be known as The Red Cube. You may remember the fuss it caused at the time, because he won it despite the fact that he was not an architect. But the accredited architect insisted Oliver share the prestigious award, and in evidence, she placed before the prize committee the initial sketch that Oliver had made. It was exactly like the final building, so they had to agree to share the prize between H. Sachs Partners and Omega Finn.

The glorious detail that made it such big news around the world was that Oliver's sketch was on a greasy McDonald's wrapper.

The wrapper is still on display in the Smithsonian Collection in Washington, DC. behind a bulletproof frame and a high railing. The number of tourist photographs of it now in existence is estimated to be only slightly fewer than those of the Mona Lisa.

The day it was installed in DC, shares of McDonalds soared worldwide and to celebrate it, they brought out the Omegaburger, a quarter-pounder on a black bun. It was their biggest seller until the tragic end of this story which, reluctantly we will have to get to later, when it was suddenly withdrawn.

However, the opening of the Final Corporation HQ building, situated in a cow pasture thirty miles from New York City, was a glorious moment, not only in the history of Omega Finn, but of New York too, and, some say, of architecture itself.

Picture this. A big green field under a blue sky. Black and white cows scattered around, munching picturesquely. In the middle of the field, a big black lake, perfectly square. And floating in the lake, a huge forty storey bright red cube. The Final Corporation Building. Massive. Just floating. Unsuspended. colossal. Red. Fantastic. Impossible. You could drive around the whole thing and wonder how in hell it could float like that. All over the world, viewers were astonished. Forty stories, red, solid, no windows. Just floating. And there was no entrance or exit. Or anything. It just floated. Unexplained. Inexplicable.

A gigantic, solid-red forty-storey cube floating in a deep black lake. Was it a real building? Or some multibillion dollar art installation?

The secret, and Oliver's great coup, was that it was partly illusion. The lake was actually only two feet deep over a black floor, but it looked infinitely deep. Above the water, it was really only half a cube of twenty stories. But the perfect reflection in the black mirror made it look like it extended as many floors below the water as above it. Half a red cube of twenty stories became a whole red cube of forty stories, floating in a deep, deep black lake. Pure illusion. Mind-blowing. Hence the Pritzker Prize.

And hence the crowds who were allowed in, to photograph it and to drive around it on a small road laid out just for that purpose, for a small entrance fee affordable by everybody, one more killer detail of the Omega Finn legend.

The actual entrance was a hundred meters away, a secret ramp down to the two floors of car-parking below the water line, hidden behind a line of hedges at the edge of the field, so that the purity of the illusion was not affected by all the comings and goings of a busy corporation. There was also a helipad on the roof of the Red Cube, serviced by the usual bright red choppers. When landing and taking off, they looked like red flies on a red sugar cube.

The helipad was for the Gang of Four; Mona, Steiner, Katsu and Di Stefano. And for Oliver and the other gypsies, of course, much to the distaste of Mona, who hated them all as much as they hated her and the other three execs. It was all sincerely mutual.

Inside the cube, the four had a meeting in Mona's big office, looking out at the green pasture and the black and white cows. Yes, there *were* windows, but they were one-way glass, invisible from outside, where the walls appeared to be a solid shiny red.

They were having a discussion. About Mona's usual subject.

- Fucking Cajuns. Fuck 'em all. We can run this without them.
- Without Oliver? C'mon, Mona. You're crazy.
- Certainly without Oliver. Kill the fucker. Dress some kid up as Omega Finn, and who's gonna know the frickin' diff? A blue kid in a white wig? Could be anybody.

Forty Two

On the side of her gaudy old caravan, 'Madame Joy' is painted in old-style carnival letters, just the way it is on her little house in the bayou. The black Harley looks at home next to it, chrome glinting in golden shades of morning as the summer sun climbs above the clouds on the horizon They both stand and stretch, a little old lady and a naked pale golden goddess side by side like two old pals, their sleepy cobwebs blasted away by the fast, windy bike ride, gazing out at the glory of it all. Madame gives Macumba's bare butt a slap.

"Go on, then. Get your crack wet."

Macumba needs no invitation. She trots out into the low surf and dives in headlong, not surfacing until she's already very far out and Madame is already a bit nervous until that golden crown bobs to the surface and they wave to each other, two babes on a lark.

'You are one nifty little fish', says Madame to herself, as she watches this angel of the jungle, raised on the river, swim away with lazy strokes into the gilded sunrise. She climbs the gaudy steps and disappears into her quirky old crib, to rustle up some bacon and eggs and some serious black coffee. Girls got a lot of talking to do.

The inside of that old caravan is like a fairyland to Macumba. Feathers, beads and bangles, funny hats and old circus posters and all the hocus pocus of the fortune teller's grift. Crystal balls, palmreaders' charts, tarot decks in velvet handkerchiefs, fancy teacups for tea-leaf reading, playing cards, jars of magic herbs, charms, ouija boards, books of spells and a real skull with fake ruby eyes. It took a good two hours of show-and-tell as they sipped a little moonshine and toked a little weed, before they got around to the real business of that summer's day. Voodoo. And Macumba's ties to it

It had not taken many turns of the cards for the old fortune teller to feel a little uneasy around the magic child. Raised in the knowledge that it was all bullshit but occasionally surprised by her own predictions, she had occasionally met with those said to have 'the shine' and been chastened by it, and by them. She ran Macumba's tarot.

- What do you see?
- Enough.

As the young wife of the Cajun who ran a traveling sideshow, Madame Joy had seen her husband knifed to death right there in front of her. Such an early lesson in loss and reality had formed the woman she now was, a mix of sweetness and steel, who fed the sparrows at her caravan but threw rocks at the 'fucking seagulls', a woman sought out for her superbly sympathetic advice, but who would interrupt a long tale of woe with, "Honey, I just wanna know who did who, and who got the two bucks."

Oliver tells the tale of her being annoyed by a pesky squirrel in her bayou house. Young Ollie suggested poisoning it, and was told off in no uncertain terms that to do such a thing would be very wrong. A month or so later they were eating one of her legendary jambalayas and he asked what this unusually delicious meat was.

- Squirrel.
- Ah. So that's why poisoning is wrong.
- It taints the meat.

Madame got straight to the point with Macumba, whose story was known to readers of celebrity mags, but which only hinted at her life as a child, the realm of black magic that she grew up in, and the rumors of a scary juju mother. It unsettled Macumba to relive it. She shook visibly at the thought of retelling what she had never told before. But here with Madame, among the harmless fakery of what to her had once been terrifying, she agreed to tell just one tale.

Macumba as a young girl. A man walks into her hut, grabs her mother, subdues her and starts to rape her. Macumba closes her eyes, summons the force she has been told she possesses and pictures the man struck dead. A snake that was coiled, unseen, in a corner, darts at him, strikes and kills him instantly, then disappears. She has never known if this was coincidence. Her mother was in no doubt.

Macumba wants nothing to do with this terrible gift. She saw how voodoo was used in her village, the curses, the vendettas and the pain. But one thing does still trouble her. Her mother's warning.

"If you don't learn how to harness this power you have, it will show itself one day and be beyond your control. And I don't want to be around when that happens."

Madame, gently taking her hand, can't help thinking mama is right.

To lighten the mood, Madame suggests they visit the Red Cube, a miles or so away. She explains that this whole area, including the little cove where the caravan is parked, belongs to the Corporation and is patrolled by men with guns, so she is quite safe living alone.

But for the visit, Macumba needs to wear something. Madame lifts the lid of a trunk holding a lifetime of old dresses. It's just like with Olaf in Manaus. And she is just as naked now as she was then.

With Macumba resplendent in one of Madame's old summer frocks, they inch the Harley around the Red Cube, joining the usual sightseers marveling at its ingenuity, this optical illusion of such a big structure seeming to float in deep black water, then they ride over to the hidden entrance and down the ramp into the building to show Macumba around, and maybe to meet the Gang of Four.

As they walk through the security door manned by a couple of scary RedEyes in full red leather gear, the dobermans are already there waiting, wagging their short tails and fawning over Macumba, licking her hands, sniffing her feet and jamming their snouts into her crotch, much to the astonishment of Madame Joy. To her, this is confirmation. How could the dogs know she was coming? It's impossible. These frightening beasts never normally leave Mona's side. Clearly, this very beautiful girl is a very special creature.

The two wander through the stylish interior, followed by the dogs, through banks of computer screens, read-outs, meeting rooms, graphic studios, up a curved stairway to the grand executive floor, checking out the big offices of the four bigwigs, especially Katsu's. It's quite a sight. On the wall is a priceless 13th Century Japanese Kendo warrior costume in full regalia, all black, the arms spread wide with a long samurai sword in one hand and the helmet with the usual mesh grill to hide the warrior's identity. It is rumored to be haunted, hence its huge value. It's known that Katsu bows to it on entering and leaving the office, to much secret ridicule from the other three bosses.

There's an angry yell from Mona as she strides out of her own huge office, enraged that her dogs have once again left her side, just like at the concert, to make a fuss of Macumba. She spits an order at them and they cringe back into her office, to get whipped.

The look Mona gave Macumba could have drawn blood.

Forty Three

Next day was Macumba's photoshoot. This was why Oliver had invited her to the concert and put her up in his Brooklyn complex. He wanted her for the next Omega Finn CD cover. She was the most famous supermodel in the world. It made business sense that she and Omega should be linked. And her being on the cover would look like she was endorsing the Omega Finn cult. Priceless.

For Oliver, a romance with Macumba was not in the cards. A carefully created rumor of romance between Macumba and Omega Finn, however, that could be very useful. But the pleasure of a real affair between her and Oliver? No. No matter how desirable she was.

But Oliver had a bit of a problem. He was starting to fall in love with her. And it would be hard to explain being seen with her if she was supposed to be Omega Finn's girl. It was a problem.

So when he arrived at her photoshoot, he was very distant with her, and said no more than a pleasant hello. He sat far from her, looking through test shots with the photographer, as she was being fussed over by hair and make-up. No chit-chat. Definitely no flirting.

He and the photographer flipped through all the test images.

- Look, Oliver. No matter how I shoot her, she looks so beautiful.

- I don't want beautiful.

- What do you want?

- I want terrified.

He got up from the lightbox and walked with the photographer to the other end of the studio where she was waiting. He put his face very close to hers and she smiled up at him in her sweet way.

He told the shooter to focus closely on her face and to press the motordrive that would click off multiple shots in split seconds, the moment he gave the signal. He bent down close to Macumba and asked her to look at him. She did so.

He yelled '*Now!*'

He slapped her across the cheek. Hard. Her face reeled from the blow, eyes wide in shock, hair flying all over. Click click click....

He got up and walked out. That was the CD cover. The title? *Nobody Is Safe.*

Forty Four

But an affair was inevitable. If Madame Joy's adoration of her Ollie and her many tales of his youth had not sold Macumba on this guy, then his own natural charm could not fail to do so, no matter how much he tried to stay away from her, and despite the famous slap that had overnight become a legend in the music biz. She hated him only for the time it took for her to understand how smart the slap had been. And anyway, she kind of liked it. A little. Not that she would say so.

Soon afterwards, in a hoodie and shades, she was walking with Madame, incognito, through the summery streets of Brooklyn, making sure Madame knew that she was against the whole cult of fear, which she knew was all fake, and the selling of the CDs as charms against bad luck. Madame let her go on, get it all off her chest, a woman with genuine voodoo power angry at the use of the fake sort just to get rich, and in the process scaring half the world.

But Madame surprised her with her reply. Suckers are suckers. Only idiots believe in the Omega Finn bullshit, anyway. Every cult is measured by the hope it generates, and they always disappoint, but Omega inverts that. Instead of hope, there's fear. And if the fear does not materialize, there's a kind of happiness. And creativity, too. Security is the enemy of creativity. On the eve of destruction, every second tastes sweeter, you get creative, doing now what you might have put off. People are now asking questions, thinking more deeply, because they fear that all this may be gone tomorrow. Which it may. They will wake from this time of fear much wiser. All because of Omega. At some point he'll disappear, set them free, and they'll look back at this time only with nostalgia.

Well, that shut Macumba up. She knew she was being conned a little. But it was all so brilliantly put. So, Madame was even smarter than she thought. And that made her feel even safer around her.

- OK. So when is Oliver going to apologize for slapping me?
- Oh, he will.
- Where is he?
- Don't worry. He'll show up.

As they turned a corner, they walked into a huge drama, an amazing sight, a real New York moment. Only in New York.

A big crowd was gathered, looking up, shouting "Jump! Jump!" Way up on a tenement roof, seven storeys high, a masked man was standing right on the edge, yelling and waving his arms around. News crews from the local TV stations were aiming their cameras at him. A bunch of guys stood in a circle, stretching a kind of net to catch him if he should jump. But the crowd just wanted action. "Jump! Jump!" they kept yelling, egging him on to maybe splatter himself on the sidewalk so they could post something ghoulish online.

The guy kept shouting something indistinguishable and a cop with a bullhorn on the street kept asking the mob to shut up so he could hear what the guy was saying. They finally shushed enough for the cop to ask the him what was going on.

- What is it, son? What are you saying?
- I said....
- What? What did you say?
- I said, I'm *bored out of my frickin' mind!!*

And with that, he jumps. Screams from the crowd. He hits the net. He bounces back up two or three storeys, then drops again and, amazingly, up he goes in the air again, but this time he does a back flip before he hits the net and up he goes again, yelling *Wheeeeee!!!!"* and does a few comical bicycle kicks and the crowd is cheering. Up and down he goes a few more times, each time doing a few more comical tricks in the air, the crowd going nuts, laughing and cheering. Clearly, the guys with the net are in on the gag, helping him to bounce on it like on a trampoline. The cop is livid with rage, yelling that they're all under arrest, and the crowd boos the cop, and finally the men with the net set the guy down on the street and scatter in all directions. The masked man runs up to Macumba, kisses her, and says to Madame, 'Hi, grandma." She laughs and says, "Hi Ollie.' before he runs off down a back alley at full tilt. The cop runs up to Madame and yells,

- What did that guy say to you?
- Go fuck yourself!
- What?
- That's what he said!

Forty Five

But this is not a romantic comedy. It's a tragedy with a heart-breaking ending. The lovers, however, did not know that when they fell in love. To them, when they fell, it was like falling into perfumed pillows.

A more romantic love affair never existed. The few details that Oliver let slip to me during our many long talks for this little book, make their romance sound like a sleigh-ride through rolling hills of sexual pleasure, a miasma of endless perfection and amazement.

A more perfect, more amazing couple you could not imagine. And they were head over heels in love with each other.

For Oliver, it was love at first meeting. Of course it was. You have to understand that Macumba was not just an adorable, funny, kind-hearted, caring and delightful little thing, 'a dimple of a girl' as one besotted interviewer put it, she was also shockingly beautiful, the supermodel of all time, a stunner who broke hearts from across the street, an angel with a face so sparklingly pretty that it was hard to look her in the eye when you spoke to her, with those pale amber irises twinkling under that aura of golden frizz on a body that was carved out of palest milk chocolate by a god with love on his mind and time on his hands, a lithe little figurine who belonged on the top of a candy box, naked until fourteen and only truly relaxed when naked ever since, thanks to the mischievous god who made her.

In fact, she was so often naked around her fellow models and make-up artists, that leaked photos of her strolling around studios happily bare-assed were everywhere, to a point where nudity almost became a fashion, a thing, a new normal. So there was little surprise when her latest *Vogue* cover was simply her standing there fully frontally nude, looking at us with those golden eyes, as innocent as the jungle.

It made history. Not because of the totally naked girl, but because it was not condemned by anyone. By no one at all. The smile was just too innocent. She was simply too sweet, too lovely, too much.

She silenced debate.

It was right after this that she posed for the Omega Finn cover. So you can imagine the tabloid shock of The Slap. We all felt it.

That *Vogue* cover became even more iconic than the one that first shot her to fame with Teetoo on her head. It spawned many serious academic studies on the subject of changing morals, the evolution of Western norms, ethnic assimilation and blah blah. But there were just as many rapturous poetic essays on the wonder of her naked beauty, one magazine writer gushing that in person she was '...just so radiantly lovely with golden hair aflame in the sunlight, that you expect little birds to alight on her bare shoulders.'

Those bare shoulders had become her signature look. They made her feel the most naked possible while clothed, she said. No one complained. Those shoulders and that neck were too beautiful for jewelry. Fragile and angular, with subtle curvatures that softened her elegant skeleton, she swanned around surrounded by admirers longing to touch the satiny velvet of her perfectly golden skin as she passed, vibrating with flagrant teenage youth.

Considering that they were the most famous people on earth, few details of their romance ever got out. They were surrounded by the band and Madame, their moat. The drawbridge was drawn up tight. So the few details that I know are the sum total of what Oliver chose to tell me in those long interviews on the phone as we got slowly bombed, conversations I tried to stretch out until he was drunk enough to spill a few more snippets and glimpses.

The love affair lasted just six months before the heartbreak and horror. But those six months were heaven, made possible by Oliver's carefully curated anonymity. Nobody knew who Oliver was. Omega was the world's biggest celebrity. Oliver was a handsome nobody.

For instance, one time in LA he was sitting on a bench across the street from Canter's Deli, listening politely to an old lady going on about money not buying you happiness. She pointed to a fat guy with two blondes in a Ferrari parked outside the deli, as an example. Oliver realized it was Di Stefano. He phoned him. Di Stefano said he was in New York, hard at work. Oliver told him to get out of the car and leave the keys. DiStefano did as he was told and stood on the sidewalk looking foolish with his two rented babes. Oliver crossed the street, got in the car, did a U-turn, asked the old lady if she needed a lift, and they zoomed off. She had no idea who he was.

So, if Oliver put shades and a hoodie on Macumba to hide that flaming crown of hair, then the pair of them could go anywhere, unnoticed, in a cloak of anonymity, a luxury beyond belief for such a famous couple. So that's what they did. They gloried in the simple pleasure of having simple pleasures. They spent a lot of time just strolling around New York, going to movies and pinball arcades, partying with the band on the roof of the Fear Building, visiting Madame Joy on her private little beach and swimming in her private little ocean, motorbiking, just being a young couple in love, ending up entwined among the mountain of pillows in the big room with the lawn and the scent of roses and the cute young Asian maid who saw much and said little, leaving them to their love and happiness.

There were, of course, special moments, particularly playful episodes. Each enjoyed making an entrance to surprise the other. Oliver more than once arrived at chic open air restaurants by parachute, as Macumba sat twiddling her thumbs, waiting. Four burly waiters once arrived at Oliver's table carrying a huge covered silver dish on their shoulders. The head waiter removed the cover with a flourish and there was Macumba, naked, with an apple in her mouth. Gasps from the diners. A silk wrap was thrown over the giggling prankster. Dinner continued.

One time, a giant Egyptian in a fez walked down the aisle of a very swell restaurant with a rolled-up rug over his big shoulder. He unfurled it dramatically on the floor at Macumba's table and out rolled Oliver dressed as Cleopatra, wig and all. Dinner continued.

Silly stunts like this wound up all over social media, but the Final Corp PR machine made sure that everybody knew that this was just Omega Finn's 'producer' wining and dining Macumba occasionally, as a friend, because Omega himself could not. He'd be mobbed if he appeared in public like that. Everybody bought it. And it was true.

Then there was the night Macumba thought she was being kidnapped, driven way out of town by a guy she didn't know, sent by Oliver, ending up in a giant scrap-metal yard, the carcasses of wrecked cars piled ten or twelve high in canyons of rusted metal. She was told to get out and she stood in a clearing, surrounded by mountains of dead motors in the dark. She was starting to freak.

But before she could get really scared, it was all flooded with lights. Carnival music blared out. From between the piles of cars marched harlequins, jugglers, men on stilts, girls on ponies riding round and round the open space, tumblers and plate-twirlers filling the place as trapeze artists flew overhead. Madame Joy, dressed in her gypsy fortune-teller outfit, rode in on an elephant. Macumba was enchanted, delighted, still a bit miffed that she'd been given such a fright, but forgiving Oliver instantly, as he walked out in a ringmaster's outfit, red jacket, high boots and top hat, grinning from ear to ear, holding in his white gloved hand an ordinary speckled hen's egg, which he cracked into her cupped palms and out spilled a pile of diamonds.

'Happy birthday,' he said.

Macumba had never had a birthday, never had a birthday party, not knowing when she was born or even how old she was. But Madame had figured, with her tea-leaves and insights that Macumba was a Leo, a summer sign, happy, confident, loyal and fun, and here on this warm summer evening, she handed her a scroll, her very own star chart, and declared tonight her twenty-first birthday. Oliver was a Scorpio, a winter sign, sexy, emotional and creative. They were made for each other, in the star books, and in life.

The band played Happy Birthday, everybody sang, Macumba cried, Madame cried, Oliver laughed and cried, everybody cried and laughed and sang and drank and danced through that hot summer New York night until dawn, when Bucket, Jones and Skins drove the couple back to Brooklyn in the Cadillac with the horns, and there never was a birthday quite like it from start to finish, from the junk-yard circus to the big mountain of pillows as the sun came up and roses filled the big room with their intoxicating sweetness.

But the exact moment Oliver fell truly in love was at the Plaza. She had complained that he always showed up looking too scruffy when she made such an effort to dress up for him. So he arrived looking immaculate, coiffed, suited and feeling a bit silly. She roared up on a Harley, dressed like a stripper, leather bikini, thigh boots, red lipstick and blonde wig. She was stopped by the outraged maitre d'. She flashed a switchblade and strolled past. All over her naked back was a huge fake tattoo that read *Middle Class Fantasy.*

That did it. He was in love before. Now he was helpless.

Forty Six

During this whole time Macumba didn't know Oliver was Omega. At first it was essential to fool her a little, for her own safety. Her questions about Omega - where was he? why could nobody meet him? - had to be deflected with harmless fibs. Oliver was waiting for the right moment to tell her, knowing that she despised Omega.

And the answers she was fed were actually true. Omega's whereabouts had to be kept secret for his own security. He performed as a hologram partly because snipers could not take out a hologram. Video showed him performing against a green screen to show that at his concerts it was all happening live and that Omega was real.

He never gave interviews because showing his face was risky. Not knowing what he really looked like without the blue face paint let him lead a more normal life. All this was true and known.

These answers satisfied Macumba, but it led to weird moments when she would ask Oliver how a lovely guy like him could work for a jerk like Omega. It made him smile but it drove him nuts. He wanted to hold her in his arms and tell her the truth, but... not yet.

Then the truth popped up by accident.

A promo of Omega was being shot in the Brooklyn basement. Oliver came to her big room afterwards. They sat out on the little lawn among the scent of roses and were served jasmine tea by the Asian maid, the kind of lovely simple moment that Macumba had come to expect with him, part of the endless fairytale.

She asked him what it was like to work with Omega. He said it was pretty easy and they left it at that. The maid split and they resumed their nonstop sexual shenanigans.

But in the middle of the usual fun and games among the mound of pillows and sheets, Macumba let out a scream. She jumped out of bed, rolled on the floor, curled up into a ball like a little girl, and started sobbing aloud. Oliver was beside himself. What could be the matter? What could have upset her so much?

Without a word, still sobbing so hard her body was shaking, she reached behind one of his ears and showed him what was on the tip of her finger. It was bright blue body paint.

What nobody knew was that around this time, Macumba was starting to feel the first stirrings of her voodoo power. She was struggling with it and losing the fight.

Uninvited and deeply unwelcome, it was starting to coil around her gentle soul like that jungle snake in her mother's hut. In fact, she had started to picture it as a snake, come to poison her from within. She could tell no one, not even Madame, the woman she trusted most in the world. She felt that if she simply ignored it, this reptile would slither away back into the dark recesses whence in came.

But it would not be ignored. It had already once reared its ugly head like a cobra, threatening, warning, but not striking. Not yet.

Not yet, but it had been a close call. It was on the night of her surprise birthday party. Just before the harlequins and jugglers had emerged from the darkness. She was momentarily terrified. In the middle of that pitch black junkyard, surrounded by those tall bleak mountains of scary automobile carcasses, not knowing what was happening, she felt herself in danger. And just as her mother had warned, the force leaped up within her like a flame-thrower.

At the very instant that the floodlights went on and the jugglers and tumblers burst from between the rusted cars, at that instant of terror, she felt blades of fire in her eyes and fingertips. For that one instant, those first few dancers could have been struck dead, blown away like ash in the wind, all of them turned to dust. She saw it like in a movie. But it didn't happen.

Her brain reacted even faster, telling her she was safe, letting her grasp the situation, the fun, the happiness of the moment. Her fires were extinguished, replaced by joy and delight. But it was so close, the line between joy and horror, that it shook her. The force had almost erupted. She had been helpless in its grasp. And she knew it.

Now, curled up like a scared infant, looking at the blue paint on the tips of her fingers, with Oliver bent over her, wishing he had told her the truth before in a gentler way, she was struggling with the power as it tried to take over again, to lash out.

As he was whispering in her ear, trying to calm her from the shock of discovering that her beloved Oliver was the loathed Omega, she was changing. She was in the process of being possessed.

Forty Seven

The Omega cult of fear had not spread to Paris. Like so many cults, it was born in the USA among the under-educated and easily fooled. In Paris, Omega was known only for his music and she had loved its sexy, funky danceable vibe. The Fear was unknown to her.

So she had been happy to pose for that CD cover. To her it was cool to be part of the music. It was only later, when she realized how very destructive it all was and how it was scaring everyone with its lies, that she turned against the whole phenomenon and began to hate Omega and all he stood for with his fake voodoo bullshit. But she adored Oliver. So she forgave him on the grounds that he was a creative guy and, well, a guy has to make a living.

But Omega Finn was repulsive to her. His cruel manipulation of the gullible with his trappings of bogus magical powers made her sick to her stomach. Even the loveable Madame Joy had not managed to sugar-coat the reality. And now that the force of voodoo was starting to gnaw her insides like a virus, her hatred was ramping up into a loathing she could not contain.

And here he was, loathsome Omega bent over her, breathing on her, not lovely Oliver but revolting Omega, incarnation of evil, the devil himself, whispering endearments, trying to worm his way into her affection, just like he had before. And she had fallen for it. Oliver was Omega! Oh my god! He had lied to her, fooled her, had made her fall in love with him just as he had seduced those millions of poor gullible Americans. Oliver is Omega! Oh my god! Oliver is Omega!

She stared in rage at those blue fingertips. She wanted to put his eyes out with them. But she gained control. Slowly. Again. With great difficulty. She forced herself to think only of Oliver, to remember that she loved him before she knew that he was also that blue devil who strutted on top of the red pyramid, humiliating and terrifying his fans, profiting from disasters. Think only of Oliver. Think only of Oliver.

He lifted her up and carried her to the bed, stroking her golden hair, caressing her golden skin. She buried her face in the pillows. She must not let him see the terrifying fires in her eyes.

They drove in silence to the Red Cube, Macumba turning her face to the car window with eyes closed, wondering what wild flames must be burning in them, flickering as they were between love and hatred, between Oliver and Omega. Oliver is Omega. Oliver is Omega.

They were driving to meet Madame Joy, the calming influence, someone Macumba could not be angry with, despite the fact that she too had withheld the awful truth about Oliver. Madame had suggested her gypsy caravan, but Oliver said his office in the Red Cube would be better with all its technology, so that he could show Macumba the whole story of how Omega Finn came into being, how they had all gotten caught up in its momentum, just a clever bit of promotion turning into something none of them could control.

He thought that with an inside view of it all, she might more easily come to terms with it, or at least understand it, so that her hatred of him at that moment might subside into the love that less than an hour ago was the center of their lives.

They arrived in silence and it stayed that way in Oliver's big office, a place he almost never visited, with its view of the fields and Macumba in a chair wearing the bathrobe he had thrown over her naked body, still curled up as she had been in her distraught fetal position with her blue fingertips.

As he talked to her gently, tenderly, apologizing for the delay in telling her the truth, explaining that he had been afraid she might leave him, knowing how much she hated the whole Omega thing. He was hoping all the while that Madame Joy would hurry up and save him from this terrible moment. Macumba just sat there staring blankly at the green fields and the black and white cows grazing out there like a strange, surreal painting, and her eyes slowly began to focus on an object on the glass coffee table in front of her. It was a steel letter opener in the shape of a dagger, long and wide enough to be a real dagger. It had the five lines of the hated Pentagraph engraved on it, an example of the many Omega Finn souvenir objects that Finnies bought in their millions to ward off possible bad luck, the fools.

It disgusted her. It embodied every aspect of cynical fakery that Omega Finn stood for. She stared at it with utter loathing.

Forty Eight

It was such a beautiful day that Madame Joy had decided to walk the pleasant mile over the fields from her caravan on the beach, instead of jumping on the Harley. She also needed time to think. She loved Macumba almost as much as she loved Ollie, and hearing his broken-hearted voice on the phone as he told her what had happened, she realized that this had to be handled very carefully if poor Macumba were not to feel betrayed.

As she approached the famous building, her heart, as always, swelled with pride at the sight, a gigantic red cube, like a kid's building block, floating as if by magic in a black lake, a cube the size of a forty storey building, half above and half below the black water, with the usual scores of sightseers amazed at its magnificence. Her Ollie had thought it all up, the Cajun boy from Mama Boo. Her eyes welled up.

And now that he had found the love of his life, nothing must get in the way of their happiness. This little bump in the road must be gotten over right away. And it was up to her to smooth their path to a love that she knew would last. She smiled to herself at the thought of being their fairy godmother, or at least a great grandmother to their kids. She quickened her step.

Inside the cube, as Oliver spoke, Macumba stared. At the dagger. She heard not a word of his tearful explanations. She heard only the fire raging in her temples at the sight of this dagger and its five lines. She was losing control. She could feel it. She was back in the junkyard among the terrifying cars. The snake was rising. She was helpless. She wanted only what *it* wanted. And it wanted to kill. To avenge. To lash out at everyone who had lied to her. Those golden irises almost spit fire as she stared at the dagger. Her hand slowly moved towards it.

Oliver saw her reach for it and saw the terrifying look in her eyes. He lunged and grasped the dagger, turned and, without even looking, he hurled it with all his strength at the door, just as Madame Joy walked through it.

The dagger slammed deep into her forehead. She was dead before she hit the floor.

Forty Nine

It was a tsunami, an avalanche of frantic media overkill. A moon-sized meteor could have destroyed half of planet Earth and nobody would have noticed, because every single TV, radio, print and online media were screaming into every microphone and banging on every keyboard on earth about the sensational mind-blowing news bombshell that was almost too huge to grasp.

Omega Finn was under arrest and in a coma at a top secret high security hospital for the criminally insane in New York, accused of murdering his grandmother, the colorful Cajun celebrity Madame Joy, his dearest friend, advisor and longtime muse.

Even more mind-blowing - if that were possible - news was now trickling out that the man everybody thought was Omega Finn was actually his 'producer', Oliver Finnegan, that it was Oliver who was in a coma accused of murder, and that Omega Finn had never existed, the deception having been a security measure for all these years.

Oddly enough, this shock revelation seemed to cause less of a stir among the millions of distraught Finnies, than the fact that their idol, whatever his true identity, was in a coma. Why? What did a coma have to do with a murder? It was driving reporters bat-shit trying to make head or tail of any of it, as were their fruitless attempts to find out where Omega was being held.

Meanwhile, under a small mountain of soft white pillows and Egyptian cotton sheets, attended by the silent young Asian maid in her crisp white uniform, Macumba lay motionless, hour after hour, silently staring at the high white ceiling, gently inhaling the scent of roses, her shallow breathing the only clue that she was still alive.

She had walked out of Oliver's office like a zombie as he lay on the floor, catatonic, next to the dead Madame Joy. She had put on his hoodie and exited the building unnoticed, just another employee, had walked until a taxi had picked her up and dropped her in Brooklyn Heights. She had walked away from the cab looking wild-eyed and completely insane. The driver had not even asked for her fare. He dared not even speak to her.

Fifty

In another white room, a room with iron bars on the window and a metal bed, Oliver lay staring at another ceiling, but staring with unseeing eyes. He was in a state of profound catatonia. They had tried every test on him, all to no avail. Although his eyes were open all the time, night and day, he saw nothing. He was simply not there. They moved him around to keep his muscles active and he allowed them to, like a rag doll. On his back he stared at the ceiling. Propped up, he stared at the five iron bars in the small window that looked onto a brick wall. He was in an intensive care unit, hooked up to an EKG machine to monitor basic functions. They were normal. But he was gone. He was far away.

This was a military facility, officially non-existent, as secret as you can get. The Gang of Four had pulled strings and greased palms to get him here under guard, with round-the-clock observation on the alert should he wake from his coma and be fit to stand trial. His lawyers, a top team assembled by Steiner, had enough juice to prod the New York Attorney General to keep his whereabouts secret and to give him time to make whatever recovery he might make. But right now any recovery looked very unlikely. Ever.

The secrecy was essential. Already, the Finnies were up in arms, holding rallies, staging marches, torching buildings, sure that their leader was being framed by the usual suspect, the Deep State.

Finnies had already stormed hospitals and prisons where they had been tipped off he might be. Social media made up conspiracies daily about him, of course. But they all led nowhere.

To the cops it was open and shut. His prints were all over the weapon, nobody else was in the room, and everybody in the place had been cleared. Even Macumba had been spoken to at Oliver's place in Brooklyn, but she was not a suspect. She had not been seen at the Red Cube that day. And anyway, she was in shock and could barely answer yes or no.

Meanwhile, the Gang of Four were watching the money roll in. Merchandise was flying off the shelves. Comatose or wide awake, guilty or innocent it didn't matter. Omega was bigger than ever.

Fifty One

Madame Joy was officially buried in the Hollywood resting place of every major movie star since the silent era and it was a funeral of biblical proportions. Mafia bosses would have been envious.

Downtown Hollywood was mobbed by Finnies who arrived by the busload, trainload and planeload. That stretch of Hollywood Boulevard known for years as Hollyweird, for the crazies who roamed it, was eclipsed by the sheer volume of insanely dressed disciples of Omega Finn who, because they all wore black, for once could not be accused of dressing inappropriately, no matter what their sartorial outrage. It was hard to take the solemn event seriously.

It looked more like Hallowe'en and was treated as such by the networks who were all there, beaming it live to the world.

But this was just the official burial, the showpiece staged for the millions watching around the globe because, knowing that the grave would be continually dug up by Finnie fanatics, it was all just a big, slightly farcical charade, and the casket was empty.

The real funeral took place down in the bayous, quietly and in secret, with just the old priest from Mama Boo and the local Cajuns. The Gang of Four were there, of course, to pretend they cared, out of place among this motley crew that they considered lowlifes.

The one glaring absentee was Madame Joy's pride and joy, the love of her long life, her darling boy, her Oliver, still in jail, blankly gazing with empty eyes at the iron bars of his window.

She was laid to rest in a pretty little stone house in the above-ground cemetary among the tall trees and the hanging moss, the catfish and the gators, just as she would have wished.

They carried her gently from her sweet and colorful old house with its painted suns and stars, her small casket swaying slowly on the shoulders of the three band member and Leo, as their former old fiddler played a sad old hymn on his gypsy violin. And so they covered the hundred yards of narrow road lined with tearful neighbors who knew to stay away and give the old girl her privacy on a day so sad and mournful and strangely poetic.

As she is carried up onto the raised ground of the cemetary, a taxi pulls up from the other direction and a slight figure in black with a long veil gets out, closes the door quietly and stands by it, The priest motions her to join the group and she follows them, a wild bunch in contrast to the four very proper executives. Few of them look like they've worn a suit except to get married in, but most manage to be in black. Some have no tie, there are a few very brightly colored shirts and various tattoos and earrings, the pride of Mama Boo, Madame Joy's nearest and dearest.

At her little mausoleum, the casket is set down and the assembly gathers around it, and as the old priest begins, 'Dearly beloved...", Bucket claps his hands once, very loud. The priest stops, and Jones whips out a big American flag and drapes it over the coffin. There's a rustle of indignation among the four corporate types, and as they step back, the small figure in black sees the draped coffin and lets out a gasp. Leo sees her face through her veil, nudges Bucket, motions with his eyes to her, and silently mouths 'Macumba'.

The priest starts again, "Dearly beloved friends of Joy Ruby Rose Felicity Finnegan..." Another loud clap from Bucket and he steps forward, cutting him off, and starts shouting to the group like an old carney barker, waving a pack of playing cards over his head.

"Pick a card! Any card!"

A rustle of surprise runs through them all as Bucket goes on in his loud voice, strutting around the casket.

"You sir! Pick a card." He fans them out. One of the Cajuns takes one. "Don't show it to me!" He continues to walk and talk.

"A deck of cards is the old gypsy bible! They tell the truth! Fifty two cards in the deck! Fifty two weeks in the year! Madame Joy was born on the eighteenth of November! That makes her the two of clubs! Smart lady. The deuce of clubs is a card of wisdom! Also a card of bad luck! Bad luck makes you smart! Good luck only makes you lucky!" A murmur of agreement passes among the locals.

He points down at the casket dramatically, "And she knows what she knows. And the truth is the truth. And a spade is a spade, no matter how you shuffle! Sir! Your card, if you'd be so kind!"

The guy gives back the face-down card to Bucket. He flips it over, holds it up high and shows it to the crowd. The two of clubs.

"And one more thing!" He lowers his arm and, holding the card at arms length he sweeps his hand around to take in all the crowd, one at a time, to include them all, especially the Gang of Four.

"Just one more thing. Never trust a bayou boy with a deck of cards!"

He throws the whole deck onto the big flag on the casket and they splay out all over it. They are all the two of clubs.

Bucket turns and leads the group out, filing slowly past the Final Corporation foursome, giving them dirty looks. Only the priest and the four executives remain, looking lost.

At the bottom of the rise, Bucket stops by the taxi as the other Cajuns file out. Macumba goes down the little hill to him and he and Leo put their arms around her. Leo says, "Don't think about it, baby. We'll nail 'em. Whoever did this better watch out."

The party breaks up and, joining the others, the two guys walk slowly back to Madame's little house, as Macumba wearily gets back in the taxi and lets it take her away, back to Baton Rouge and to the airport and to whatever comes next. She gazes out of the window and sees nothing. The man she loves is in prison, his mind frozen in some psychotic void. Her newest and dearest friend and confidante is dead.

And she did it. All of it.

In another taxi headed for the same airport where a private jet awaits, the Gang of Four are having very different thoughts about the Cajuns, all of them having been treated at the funeral with such scorn by what they consider the scum of Louisiana. They trade thoughts.

- Madame Joy? Screw her. Good riddance. Bucket, Jones and Skins? Easily replaced.
- Leo. He's a problem. A genius. Unique. Irreplaceable. And filthy rich already. This might require some strong-arm tactics.
- Oliver? Ha! He's toast. History. Even if he comes out of his coma, his days are numbered. Paint some kid blue, get some copywriters with no conscience from Mona's old advertising agency to write spooky Omega Finn songs and... phttt! so long, sucker.
- But it was weird, him killing his grandma, eh? What was that all about? Oh, who gives a shit, anyway. Goddam swamp scum!
- And where's that Brazilian bitch off to, now her boy's in jail?

Fifty Two

That Brazilian bitch was off to Brazil.

From the funeral, she flew to Paris, to ward off insanity with Fabien.

Inwardly she was hysterical. She knew exactly what she had done. She had lost control of her voodoo power, had ignored its growing threat and had failed to harness it as her mother had warned her. She had not listened. Like a fool she had wanted it simply to go away. Like a fool she had ignored it and ignored what she had been told repeatedly by her mother and by the old women in Manaus - that she was chosen. She was gifted. It was not up to her to want or to not want. It was in her. She had to live with it, to feel it and, with time, to direct it.

But now that it had shown itself to be her master, with horrific results, maybe now it was too late. Was it? She had to find out.

Fabien was her gentle savior once again. She did not tell him of her direct involvement in Madame's death, just that voodoo was swirling around her and she felt implicated. He listened, understood. and sympathized. Even more important, he knew voodoo. He knew how deadly serious the situation was that Macumba was in. He and Olaf had combed the Amazonian jungle for years to study languages and artforms, but also voodoo, juju, candomblé, all the names and forms of the dark power that was as real as the power of the river.

After many long days of calming talks and long evenings of good wine and of sleeping next to Fabien to ward off the nightly nightmares, Macumba, hooded and anonymous with him, boarded the same flight in reverse that had brought her from Manaus to Paris a lifetime ago.

They were going to see Olaf. They were going to try to unwind the clock, to unlive her recent life, to untwist the voodoo spiral, to follow the great Rio Negro river back upstream to the old man in the treetop, to the old women she had slipped away from in Manaus, to beg forgiveness and to sit at their feet and listen, finally, to their wisdom. And then, if such a thing might be possible, they were going to go with Olaf and a crew of the best river men armed with all the new devices and GPS locators, to try to find the place she had been swept away from in that terrible flood, on a log with Teetoo, to find her tribe again and finally, possibly, to meet her mother.

At Manaus, where the vast Rio Negro runs fast, dark and deep, Macumba, Olaf and Fabien with a small crew of river men in two flat metal boats, narrow and shallow to allow them to navigate small streams in their search for her lost tribe, rode them upstream against the current on this roiling giant, holding on like on bucking broncos.

After turning into a lesser river, then into other smaller ones with gentler currents, on the third day Olaf guided them to the bend in the river where the old Englishman in his treetop first saw Macumba on her log, naked and half dead. There was a tearful reunion at the return of the magic child, and the old ladies asked forgiveness for their kidnap attempt. Through Olaf, they repeated their certainty of Macumba's juju power, begging her to be more respectful of it.

Macumba needed no persuading. She was terrified of it.

On the next stretch upriver, the banks are steeper, the boats hemmed in by jungle, everyone wondering if arrows are about to fly at them from the green walls on either side. The local crewmen keep up loud chatter with the silent trees, in many dialects, as they pass tribe after tribe, so that those hidden on the riverbank will know that they are not raiding parties, just harmless hunters passing through.

These protocols of the river keep the poisoned arrows sheathed.

In the humid hothouse of these backwaters, simply not passing out from the hammering heat is itself a victory, as the metal boats crawl along and the crews call to each other to avoid hidden shoals and sandbanks that could overturn them and feed the piranha.

Olaf navigates via languages, into areas with dialects similar to Macumba's. But in a week they are as lost as they dare get, relying on GPS, flying a drone to look for smoke rising from the canopy. Days go by. They go deeper than Olaf or Fabien have ever dared to go into the deep unknown, with Macumba in the first boat looking for things that might spur a memory, shouting her strange words into the green walls, the slim boats almost touching the banks on either side and the crew about to mutiny out of pure terror.

Then a crack! A scream! A mob of yelling naked men crash into the water, hemming the boats in, squealing and fighting to drag her out of the boat, and she's yelling at them and talking to them. She's talking to them. *She's talking to them!* She's home.

Fifty Three

What a world. What a tribe. What a welcome. What a week.

Macumba dances naked and golden in a circle of darker naked men all garlanded in white orchids, as they roll their heads to the drum's rhythms, lost in a communal hallucination, blue feathers in their hair, torsos in red zigzags, lost in one more dance to summon the dark power.

She looks so different from the others. Surrounded by her naked village, her unique looks jump out like a flame in a dark room. To her village she is as extraordinary as she is to her admirers in Paris.

She is an entirely different color. The secret of those pale amber eyes, gold skin and hair is that she is a rare form of albino mutation seen here in a rare generation and, they believe, the source of the juju that threatens her life because she has no control over it. The unique beauty this has given her is astonishing, even to her own people.

Olaf and Fabien sit off to one side with Macumba's proud mama, she and Olaf trying to talk in the clickety-clack language. But the two of them have already spoken at length, with Macumba translating. All that needed to be said has been said, all unknowns known.

This communal trance is the climax to a week of rituals to beg the dark snake to live in harmony with its lovely host.

Her childhood killing of the rapist is legend here. She was always magic, her return a miracle. There has been a river baptism, a fire-walk, ritual body painting, a screaming exorcism by the women, eyes rolling back in their heads, the smoking of a pipe the size of a pail, passsed among the men, at which the ghost of Madame Joy appeared, which left Macumba weeping pitifully until it disappeared into the blue smoke. It has been a sacred festival and a stoned jamboree, more fun than solemn. Jungle juice has flowed, the whole village tripping for a week.

Jungle juice. Ah. A great name for a band. Or for the evil hooch they brew in all the villages up and down the Amazon, each tribe with its own recipe. But among explorers, adventurers and intrepid souls who have drunk it for research or just to be polite, whatever the recipe, it has always had the same wicked nickname, said with a wince at the memory.

Olaf and Fabien are no strangers to its brain-twisting charms.

It starts out as cassava, a sweet potato that is the main crop around here. Macumba calls it a name with clicks that Olaf can't pronounce. Served with fish in a gourmet Havana restaurant, you'll find it quite memorable. In Macumba's village you'll never forget it.

First, the women chew it and spit it into a big dugout log. Then they add the entrails of critters that look like rats and *are* rats. Then comes a foul-smelling fungus that from a distance you might mistake for a backed-up toilet. Then they leave it out in the open, far away from the village, because even they can't stand the stink.

The yeasts that floats around in the humid primal soup that is the air around here, cause it all to bubble and plop and ferment for a week or so until it is strong enough to stagger a yak. Then it's your turn.

But before being poured into coconut shells for your delectation, there's one more tiny *coup de grace* of the distiller's art. A little naked girl is lifted high above the shimmering brew and, smiling her sweet smile, she pisses into it. That's the cherry on top, so to speak.

- That used to be me.

- Really, Macumba? They drank your piss?

- Even then, I was the chosen one. Even then, they knew.

- Do we *have* to drink this?

- Fabien, you are the honored guests.

Olaf grins at Fabien. They have been here before. They roll their eyes. They know what is about to happen to their brains. And it does.

And now at the end of this week of wonders, with everyone still tripping out of their minds, her mother steps into the circle of this last big communal dance and leads her beautiful girl by the hand into her hut, the same hut where first Macumba felt her power and killed the man who tried to rape her mama.

She sits her down, places a painted stick in her hand and a tray of river mud on the floor in front of her. Still in a total trance from the dance, not knowing what she does, Macumba draws five straight lines, one above the other, then opens her eyes and, with a gasp, sees what she has drawn. It was unconscious. It is the Pentagraph.

In Oliver's prison room, as he stares with dead unseeing eyes at the five horizontal bars of his window, they suddenly glow white hot. The image sears his brain. He blinks. He wakes from his coma.

Fifty Four

Manaus can be quite a beautiful place, if you have money.

Fabien arranged for Olaf to join Macumba and himself as once again they boarded the *Grand Amazon* at the upstream end of its cruise. They sailed langorously and affluently down the Rio Negro, to arrive in Manaus scrubbed clean of all the ticks and fleas they had hosted in the jungle among the lost tribe that they promised would stay lost.

Parting was painful. Both Macumba and her mother were hysterical. It was hard to tell who was the more broken-hearted. They tried several times to push away from the riverbank before either Macumba jumped back out of the boat or her mother jumped into it. But the final parting was smoothed by Fabien's persuasive altering of goodbye to *au revoir.* They would be back. They had the GPS record, so they could retrace the zigzag route. And they all did want to retrace it, especially Olaf. He had found a new language with a whole new level of 'lost'.

It had taken over a week to find the tribe, and a week to revel in its glorious welcome. But the return was downstream, and the crew thrashed those old engines, fairly surfing down the rivers from smaller to bigger to biggest of all, bringing the trio to the *Grand Amazon* in only a couple of days, getting a huge cash bonus, a kiss from the prettiest girl in the world, and the memory of seeing her dance naked for hours on end in her trances, reward enough for any red blooded sailor.

In Manaus, at Olaf's college digs, there was a video reunion with Oliver. Macumba wept helplessly, knowing that her moment of magic in her mama's hut had sprung him from his psychic trance, but unable to say so, because Oliver, the great faker of voodoo, still did not believe in the real thing. He still remembered nothing of the killing. So she decided not tell him what she knew, merely agreeing with him that he was incapable of doing such a thing and leaving it a mystery. She did so with a sigh of relief. Their perfect love affair could resume. She was relieved and very happy.

She hoped that, thanks to mama's teachings, the evil juju would never again rise in her, that she would never again feel as helpless as when she learned that Oliver was Omega. But she knew it was still only a hope.

Fifty Five

Oliver was awake but remembered nothing. The entire episode of the killing was gone from his mind. In fact, one of the first things he did after waking was to ask to see Madame Joy.

Telling him what had happened had to be done with the utmost care. To ready him, his doctors gave him enough downers to slow a racehorse. Even so, when they told him the details, it almost put him back in a coma.

After hearing the full horrific story, it was many days before he could get out of bed or eat or drink or function in any way. And still he remembered nothing. Even their detailed account seemed incapable of opening that locked door. The cops only wanted to know if anybody had been in the room with him when Madame Joy was killed, but it was pointless to even ask. It was a dead zone in his head. A void. Every test they gave him proved that he was not faking it. The amnesia was total and for real and seemed permanent.

But the authorities had bigger things to worry about. Street riots with armed gangs of Finnies roaming the streets, were turning protests into riots, almost all-out civil war. The media took sides. Either you thought the Finnies were misinformed morons or you agreed with them that this was all a nationwide conspiracy to get rid of Omega Finn. Even the revelation that Oliver was Omega was seen as just more Deep State propaganda. Things were coming to a head. It was escalating. The police were over-stretched. There was talk of calling in the army.

Oliver's lawyers fanned the flames, of course, by insisting that the evidence was purely circumstantial. And they had a point. His prints were all over the murder weapon, yes, but of course they were. It was his own letter opener. He used it every time he was in his office. It proved nothing.

A meeting was held between the Gang of Four and Oliver in his high-security facility. Homeland Security officials, along with the military and police were patched in on scrambled video feeds across the country, all trying to figure out how to bring Oliver to trial without setting off a nationwide riot. They released video clips showing that Oliver was still alive, and being treated well by the authorities. That calmed things down a little. For a while. But the days-long meeting was getting nowhere. The whole country was on a hair trigger.

And with social media whipping up the mess with its usual helpful lies, pretty soon civil war was seriously in the cards.

Something had to be done, short of releasing Oliver, to appease the mobs and diffuse the gathering storm, since now *anti*-Finnie groups were being formed to help the police fight the Finnie mobs and pretty soon they were as scary as the Finnies themselves and, this being the land of the free, every one of them was armed to the teeth with the kind of perfectly legal weapons you could invade Europe with.

At the point when it seemed nothing could stop the conflagration and with everyone jacked up on the same chemical crank as the Finnies, one bright person in the big meeting had a brainwave.

A free concert. That might do it. An Omega Finn free concert would give everybody a reason to *not* start torching and looting cities and killing each other in droves. It might even be something to look forward to and something to talk about that didn't involve butchery.

A negotiated solution was reached. Oliver would be tried behind closed doors before a Grand Jury, avoiding a public circus. But first, he would go on camera and admit to being Omega, while claiming no memory of the killing. His lawyers would plead not guilty and with only circumstantial evidence against him, they might even get him off. But he would give the free concert, whatever the verdict, even if he was officially still under arrest, details to be decided later.

The nation exhaled. The concert was on. The teeshirt went on sale.

And it worked. The promise of a concert got everyone excited. Oliver was convincing on TV, bringing his considerable charm to bear explaining why it had been necessary to pretend to be Omega. It all turned into such a love fest that he even got children to paint his face blue on camera. Forgiveness for the Oliver-Omega deception was total.

The Finnie gangs and *anti*-Finnie gangs agreed to stand down during his trial, awaiting the verdict. But the not-guilty verdict was starting to look very likely.

Meanwhile Oliver, still in custody, was required to name a power of attorney to sign all documents on his behalf while he was locked up. It was assumed that he would name the company lawyer, Di Stefano. To the absolute horror of the Gang of Four, he did not.

He named Macumba.

Fifty Six

After Manaus, Macumba flew to LA to stay with Leo. A level head. Fabien joined them in the Topanga Canyon palace. A calming influence.

The three were in constant touch with Leo's lawyers and with Oliver, who was given full internet access via a military satellite.

As Oliver's power of attorney, Macumba was now in control of many things, not least of which were many billions of dollars, piling up daily as Omega Finn merchandise ramped up to a new frenzy and The Final Corporation grew richer than most American banks.

The band laid low in the Fear Building, well, as low as three comical nuts could lay, shooting down drones with assault rifles from their famed New York rooftop and spawning a video game based on the new sport.

Oliver and Macumba were missing each other like crazy. They were making secret plans to get together for a few hours despite the military lockdown. The bribes to the grunts on jail duty ran into the millions of dollars per soldier. But, hey, who's counting?

Who *is* counting when there's just so much money sloshing around? The Omega Finn cult was already the wealthiest 'church' in the world and Oliver the richest human. The money was beyond sick. For instance, when Macumba had flown to LA to be with Leo, she just rolled up to a hanger at Kennedy Airport in a red helicopter with two big suitcases full of $100 bills, and left in an empty Boeing 777 with flight attendants bribed from various airlines, and a flight crew in their underwear, dragged from their hotel beds and given a gram of coke each to wake them up.

It's hard to imagine wealth on this level because neither Oliver, Leo nor Macumba cared for money, and the band couldn't give a shit. When they traveled they may rent an entire airliner, yes, but when they arrived, they would just crash with other buddies and work on cars.

The Gang of four on the other hand were total greed heads. They just worshipped money and acquired everything they could see. And they were sure Macumba would turn off the cash tap as Oliver's power of attorney. They met in a row boat on the Central Park lake, scared of being bugged.

- That bitch is walking around playing the queen.
- But what can we do, Mona?
- We can play the ace.

Fifty Seven

The death of Madame was the end of The End.

Oliver didn't want to be Omega Finn any more. It had all been the pure invention of Madame and Oliver, a piece of brilliant conceptual art. The pinnacle of rock idolatry. An actual religion! Such power and influence! For a pair of smart cookies from the Atchafalaya swamp to take over the world like that? Astonishing. No wonder they allowed it to get too big and too scary to control. It was a work of genius.

But the joy of it was Madame Joy. To sit with heads together, the hip young rocker and the wise old bird, and come up with the next wild idea and the next, *that* was the joy of it. Always had been. And now she was gone... he wanted it all to go away. He missed her so badly.

Macumba and Leo agreed with him. They should pull the plug.

But how? There were still many millions out there who actually believed Omega Finn was a god with the power to prevent disasters. How to make folks un-believe? Faith is a tattoo on the brain. Indelible.

In the Red Cube, the Gang of Four were having a very different heart to heart. A heartless one. The turn of events had made it nearly impossible for them to get rid of Oliver and the Cajuns. And now Macumba had Oliver's power of attorney. She'd do whatever he wanted and he wanted to end it. The only way to stop her turning off their cash tap was to turn her against Oliver. And that was impossible.

Or was it? Mona still had that ace up her sleeve. But how to play it?

Mona was a fine looking woman, red hot, in her 40s, athletic and, if pussy-whipping milfs are your thing, a world champion. She had her way with every cute guy at her advertising agency in the days when to accuse a woman of sexual harassment was a joke. If you didn't want to get fired, you had to bend her over her big teak desk whenever she hiked up her short skirt and showed you she wore nothing underneath.

It was all part of the gig. She was the boss. And if you wanted to get ahead, you did the right thing. You did the boss.

And one of the cute young guys she had basically forced into having sex with her in the early days of The Final Corporation, was one of the main reasons she took the job in the first place. Oliver.

And she had recorded it. All of it. As usual. Well, it was her thing. To watch herself getting serviced by a string of likely lads gave her hours of solo viewing pleasure. At the time, Oliver was just another stud on the reel, perfectly oblivious, never suspecting there were cameras all over her office, recording him from every angle. She wanted optimum effect. She was a pro, after all, and her sex tapes were as polished as the TV commercials she produced in her ad agency.

Scrolling through her greatest hits, locating the legendary rockstar Omega Finn with his Levis around his ankles, Mona could reflect with a certain pride that it was every bit as smooth as any online porno.

More to the point, she had the facilities right there to re-edit it in a way that would show Macumba a story very different from the way it had really happened. The Omega sex tape would no longer be just another chapter in her private pervert's library. It would be ammunition.

And the target was an easily-heart-broken Brazilian bimbo who had the power to screw up Mona's wealth with her goddam power of attorney.

What could be easier? She would re-edit it so that Oliver seemed to be the predator, not her. Worse, she would make it look as if it was still going on, not finished after one quick office bang years ago, as it had been. Oliver had only done it to help smooth their professional relationship right at the start. He was just being a nice guy, to let her have her way and not hurt her colossal vanity, that's all. Just the once.

But when Mona was done with it, it would look very different.

She decided to act as if she really didn't want to show this 'painful episode' to Macumba, but felt compelled to, woman to woman, to show her that Oliver was not as devoted to her as she thought, but just a cold-hearted two-timing jerk, like all men. She could hardly wait.

Macumba had just landed from L.A. and she accepted the invitation to meet in Mona's office. It all went without a hitch. Mona acted very sad to have to present her with evidence of Oliver's treachery. Macumba said nothing, but slipped the small external drive into her jeans pocket. She said she'd watch it later, and left.

Mona buzzed Di Stefano.

- We got her. Stupid bitch.
- Great. And look at the date, Mona. It's April first.
- I know. April Fool's Day.

Fifty Eight

The keys to Madame Joy's Harley with the chrome Springer front forks, were always right there on the tank, since nobody would ever dare steal it. Macumba fired it up and did a full-lock one-point U-turn just as Madame had taught her in those parking-lot lessons. She ran it up the ramp and out of the Red Cube into the crisp spring night. It was the night of the April full moon, and as she rumbled gently over the meadows to the gypsy caravan on the water's edge, she took in the shapes of the cows lying down in the moonlit field, chewing their cud. She took it slow, to savor the cool evening and to give herself time to calm down before the freezing nude swim she'd promised herself. The April Atlantic is ice cold and that's just how she wanted it. Needed it. She was livid. On fire.

The flames were rising in her. If she had not turned and walked out of Mona's office back there, she might well have tried to strangle the bitch. The slimy fake concern as Mona told her about her 'affair' with Oliver and how he was still obsessed with her and still came to her office and forced himself on her and... blah blah, all with those fake tears welling in her reptile eyes. If it were not for those two sweet dogs staring at her lovingly, she would have smashed her face in with her big desk phone.

As if she didn't already know what Mona was 'revealing' to her, the lying whore! Oliver had told her about it long ago and had even managed to get a copy of the tape, just to come clean with her, to make sure that something like this never happened to her, knowing Mona as he did.

They had watched it together, laughing at Mona's corny idea of sexy seduction and Oliver's awkward reluctance. It had been a sweet moment between them. Now maybe she would watch it again, just to crank up her hatred of the bitch who was now her sworn enemy.

But she must be calm. Anger was her enemy. Her anger had killed. The full moon, rising in the East, was reflected in the ocean, making a silver ribbon of light from where Macumba stood, naked and shivering, all the way to the clear horizon. She ran into the shining pathway and dived in. She swam with an energy born of violent hatred and was half a mile out before she pulled up, spent and calmed, and then turned and carved a lazy furrow all the way back to the old painted caravan, lit up like a toy house in the silver light of the Spring full moon.

Swathed in towels, she slid Mona's file into Madame's laptop and lay back, hair wet and salty, surrounded by the fairyland of familiar objects that had belonged to her beloved old friend, shuddering at the memory of what her rage had done to this beautiful woman and weeping quietly at the memory of it. She recalled her mother's advice about controlling her rage, balancing her normal self and her voodoo self, to accept, not fight, what cannot be beaten. Helpless vessel of voodoo or calm user of it, was the choice. The trigger was her anger. It had no off-switch.

But then she hit Play, and her good intentions flew out the window.

The sex tape had been completely re-cut. Mona had edited the scene in a sickening new way that was all lies. No longer was she leaning naked against her desk as Oliver walked in looking awkward, ordering him to get his sweet ass over to her and do her bidding. On the original tape she had leaned against her desk in her high heels and made him say violent things to her that had almost made him laugh. But now she had moved the soundtrack to later in the tape, where she was now bent over her desk with Oliver behind her, so that it sounded like Oliver was *now* saying those same violent words to her that she had forced him to say earlier. It looked more like rape.

Macumba's brain nearly exploded.

She grabbed the laptop and slammed it onto the floor, destroying it. She was screaming with hatred in her jungle language at this evil, lying, manipulative bitch who was trying to tear her and Oliver apart so she could continue the cult of fear that Macumba hated with all her soul and which she and her friends had decided to bring to an end. The woman was evil! She had to be stopped! They all had to be stopped! This whole sick corporation had to be torn down for ever!

She ran naked out of the warm old caravan into the cold night air, falling to her knees in the sand, screaming wild Amazonian curses at the sky, howling like a she-wolf at the full moon. She was lost. She was gone. The eyes rolled back in her head. She was totally helpless again, gripped by the voodoo. Village drums beat in her ears. The snake had risen in her like a cobra. She slumped down, staring at nothing. Her hand landed on a sliver of driftwood. In her trance, on her knees, she grabbed the stick blindly. Beyond all conscious thought, she started to make a mark in the sand.

Fifty Nine

Over the fields in the Red Cube, all four of the Gang Of Four in their big offices are all feeling pretty good about the new turn of events. Mona has quite possibly pulled off a coup that had seemed impossible a few days earlier when they were having their paranoid pow-wow in that row-boat and wondering if Macumba might be about to dissolve the Final Corp on Oliver's orders. Gone would be Di Stefano's Ferraris and hookers, Katsu's private army, Steiner's private island, and whatever sick sex Mona got up to with her money, probably involving entire football teams.

Now it all looks rosy again. A full moon on April First and all's well.

As the evening darkens, a couple of distant coyotes start to howl at the full moon. The dobermans join them, occasionally howling like wolves themselves. It amuses Mona, but Steiner freaks and insists she let the dogs out to howl elsewhere. Which she does. Their howling adds a darkly gothic note to the gathering gloom in the moonlit fields.

Katsu, leaving his grandiose office for the evening, turns off all the lights except the small spotlight that is always lit, illuminating the Kendo warrior with its arms spread-eagle, holding the equally rare, and razor sharp samurai sword in its right gloved hand. In the open doorway, he bows to it with reverence, as usual, closes the door gently and takes the elevator down to the basement garage.

On the beach, naked and staring blindly at the full moon in a total trance, Macumba makes a mark with her stick. A horizontal line.

Mona suddenly sits bolt upright in her office, and says aloud, "Oh, what a great idea!" She gets up, rushes out and strides with purpose down the wide carpeted hall of the VIP floor.

On the beach Macumba, entranced, entirely unaware of her actions, draws a second horizontal line above the first one.

Di Stefano suddenly stops dead as he is walking through the VIP floor, clicks his fingers as if he's just had a great thought, turns around, walks to Steiner's office, opens the door, leans in and yells, "Yo, Steiner!"

He says he has something to show Steiner and it's up on the roof. Steiner reluctantly allows himself to be dragged into the elevator.

- You're taking me to the roof? Why the roof? What the hell is this?
- A surprise, buddy. Loosen up. You're gonna love this.

On the beach, Macumba makes a third horizontal line under the other two. In her trance, like in her village, she is drawing a Pentagraph.

In the basement garage, Katsu settles into the black leather driver's seat of his custom Lamborghini, bright red of course, buckles up, leans forward and starts the engine. The soft growl of the V-10 puts a smile on his face and he leans back to savor the sound. Then the phone rings. It breaks the blissful mood. He hits a button and barks 'Yeah! What?"

- Mr Katsu. Please come back to your office right away.
- Whu? What for? Who is this?
- It's most urgent, Sir. You must come back immediately.

The phone clicks off. He yells a couple of filthy Japanese curses and wearily unbuckles, gets out, and walks back to the elevator.

On the chilly, breezy roof, Di Stefano is standing next to a big archery target, beaming with satisfaction.

- One of my girls got it for me. Isn't it great? It's Olympic size.
- I don't give a speckled hen fart. It's cold up here.
- Because you ain't seen nothin' yet, Steiner. Check out this little puppy.

He removes from its case a beautiful inlaid antique French crossbow.

- Ah. Yes. Now, *that* really is a fine piece, I'll admit. A rare piece.
- I knew you'd love it. You place the arrow in it like so.
- They're called darts, not arrows, you dumb bastard.
- See! I knew you were an expert. But don't stand so near the edge.
- I used to win medals at this. One of these will kill you, you know.
- So be careful. It's on a hair trigger. Not so close to the edge, huh?
- I know what I'm doing. I just wish those dogs would quit howling.

On the beach, Macumba makes the fourth line in the sand.

Katsu arrives at his office, opens the door and stands there, dumbstruck. The Kendo warrior is not on the wall. It is standing on his desk, facing him, sword grasped in its two hands. Katsu nearly faints from fright. But he knows exactly what to do. He has read the books about ghost warriors. Slowly he kneels before it and bows his head respectfully. The warrior jumps and lands right in front of him with a loud "Huunh!"

Katsu jumps forward, grabs the sword from the warrior's hands, sweeps it back in a high arc and, grunting with effort, slams it deep into the belly of the ghost warrior.

In the field, the two dogs suddenly look up and snarl at the Red Cube.

Katsu, with all his strength, pulls the embedded sword upwards through the warrior's belly and to the side, the classic move of *Seppuku,* or Harakiri, the noble suicide of the devoted samurai, exactly as it should be done with ghost warriors, according to Katsu's antique books.

He pulls out the sword and looks at it. To his total shock, it is covered in blood. Real blood. The warrior, still standing, staggers and its intestines fall out of its belly and splash onto the floor in a glistening pink heap in front of Katsu. He's totally bewildered, looking down at them. The warrior falls to its knees, keels over sideways and hits the floor. As it hits the floor the black mesh helmet is knocked off, revealing the face. It is Mona.

She looks up at him with dying eyes and whispers, "April Fool."

On the beach, Macumba makes the final line of the Pentagraph.

In the field, the dogs leap forwards and race to the Red Cube, slam through their dog door, tear up the stairs three at a time, floor by floor and crash into Katsu's office, leaping for his throat, hurling him to the floor and ripping him apart like a rag doll, as he lets out a terrified, helpless scream so loud that it echoes through the building.

On the roof, Di Stefano stands proudly right in front of the target, hands on hips, as Steiner, crossbow in the shooting position, suddenly jumps at the terrifying scream, accidentally pulls the trigger, stumbles back at the recoil and falls over the edge, tumbling twenty storeys down to the black lake below and slamming into the water like it's concrete.

On the roof, Di Stefano looks down at his chest and the dart that has just gone right through him. He slumps over, instantly dead, impaled on the target by a perfect shot into the bullseye.

On the beach, Macumba slowly leans backwards onto the cool sand, spent of all energy, stick in hand, staring up at the dark night sky and the full moon and lets out a long sigh as she slowly wakes from her trance, entirely unaware of what she has done.

She walks, shivering, back to the caravan where she slides under the warm covers of Madame Joy's old ornamental iron bed and falls instantly fast asleep.

Outside, on the edge of the ocean, small wavelets lap slowly over the sand and over her Pentagraph, erasing it entirely.

Sixty

The quadruple murder-suicide, or whatever the hell it was over there at the Red Cube, broke the Internet and choked all media for a good month after the event. But whichever of the various possible scenarios the cops managed to come up with to explain this incomprehensible wild bloodbath, the last thing anybody mentioned was voodoo. It never even made it onto the list. And Macumba was not there. So she was off the hook. She was fast asleep in Madame Joy's old seaside caravan, a mile from the scene of the crimes, with the two dobermans asleep at her feet, when the cops got around to searching the whole area the following day.

She was shocked speechless by what they told her, clearly unaware. She flew back to LA with the dogs, who were not deemed dangerous as they had obviously just defended Mona and then in their distress, sought out Macumba, their favorite person. Leo and Fabien both loved the dogs, so they settled right in and just added to the family feel of Leo's place.

The wild events had the collateral effect of freeing Oliver. As soon as the details of this bloody mess were made public, the once-bizarre killing of Madame Joy suddenly looked tame by comparison. And since Oliver had absolutely nothing to do with this one, then clearly he had nothing to do with the other one, obviously just an innocent witness to the crime, sent into an amnesiac coma by the sight of what he had seen. Which was the exact truth. His lawyers, using a massive public outcry as leverage, had him out and free of all charges in a few days. So he too went to Topanga Canyon and there was a tearful reunion followed by a long discussion of what they should do next.

Macumba gave no hint to Oliver, Leo or Fabien about her role in all this. She remembered nothing, but she knew it had to be her doing, recalling her rage at Mona. She was now in a constant state of fear. Afraid of herself.

The shock events also had the effect of putting the whole Omega Finn cult into question among its own disciples. A quasi-religion run by such scary, murderous lunatics was not exactly a good basis for belief. Add to that the fact that Omega had admitted that he did not really exist, and the seeds of an inevitable entropy were starting to be sown among even the most loyal of the faithful. Sales of the CD slowed.

Sixty One

So what about the free concert? It had been promised in haste, to stop riots. But now that Oliver was out, exonerated, riots were moot. All attention now was on the sick mystery of the Gang of Four slaughter. Social media, conspiracy nuts and fake news hounds went bat shit.

But all were agreed in wanting an Omega Finn concert. And now that the Gang Of four were all dead and the Omega cult winding down somewhat, Oliver wanted it, too, a stage for him to announce his retreat from the spotlight, to clear up a few things with fans, a confession of sorts, officially ending The Fear, closing the books on a reign of terror and, most of all, bidding a grand farewell to his beloved Madame in the hope that everybody would finally get the message that they should forget The Fear and get on with their lives after this final concert, the final act of The Final Corporation.

So, Leo and Oliver had a lot of thinking, sketching and creating to do in Leo's techno wonderland on the mountain top, and it was a very pleasant time for everyone, coming after such horror and pain.

Macumba spent a lot of time walking with Fabien and the dogs on the Topanga hills, reminiscing over their time in the jungle. They decided to keep all that jungle stuff to themselves. It might spook Oliver to hear about it, as he still didn't fully believe in any of it.

And anyway, as far as Fabien and Olaf knew, the trip up the Rio Negro, the lost tribe and the long talks between mother and daughter were all just a desire of Macumba's to re-connect with her past and to seek the lost years that had been snatched from her by the flood. Neither Fabien nor Olaf knew that she was the cause of Madame's death or the multiple murders that followed, or that she had already become a voodoo channel. That was for mama's ears only, and even she didn't know the whole story, which was Macumba's lonely cross to bear.

A welcome arrival at Leo's place was the band. They showed up from their usual good time in Mexico, to add to the family feeling, drinking beer and playing poker with Leo and Ollie for hours.

The three guys were playing poker together one day when Macumba walked in with the dogs

"Pick a card! Any card," Bucket yelled, holding out the pack. She pulled the two of clubs. "Not funny," she said, her eyes welling up.

Bucket was bewildered. He had not intended that to happen.

- No. I didn't do that, Macumba. Pure chance. You just picked it.

- Oh bullshit, Bucket. That's so cruel. Here. Give me another.

Macumba reached down to the proffered pack and pulled out another card. Another two of clubs. She started crying and cursing Bucket, and pulled another two of clubs, then another and another, all of them the two of clubs, and threw them all at him, calling him a cruel bastard and left the room crying, slamming the door behind her.

Bucket looked around at the other guys in a kind of horror. He turned over the rest of the pack and threw them onto the table. There were no more two of clubs among them. It was just an ordinary pack of cards. They all stared at the pack and at each other in silence. Skins picked up his phone. "Leo? Get in here. Just get in here right now."

They told Leo what happened. Bucket showed him the cards. Jones sat everybody down and ran the situation down.

- We all saw this happen. Ollie doesn't believe in this shit. But we grew up around Madame, and she explained it all. We have open minds about it, right? This girl has that thing. What did Madame call it?

- The shine.

- The shine. She's got it, sure as shit.

There were long silences in that room. Nobody wanted to say what they thought. They all loved Macumba. But she was a child of the jungle, after all. And those deaths? All of them so weird. The murder of Madame, like a ritual killing. And where was Macumba at that moment? Oliver couldn't recall anybody else being in the room. But he could recall nothing else, either. Could they jolt his memory? Give him some kind of shock? Shock it out of him? The silences went on. It was a long, heavy moment. Skins said forget it. Let's play cards.

They sat around and played in silence and drank, letting the whole thing percolate, slosh around in their brains a little. But they could not think straight. At some point, Leo undid the rubber band tying back his long grey hair. It fell over his face like a grey curtain. Jones lifted it up.

- How the fuck can you see through that shit, you hippy?

Leo laughed and stuck it behind his ears and dealt cards to the others. But Skins gave Leo a long, strange look and put his beer down.

- Guys. I got an idea.

Sixty Two

The band drove down with Oliver, from the Canyon into Malibu in a big old convertible, for a swim in the ocean, a change of scene. They were cruising along Pacific Coast Highway, Bucket driving, Oliver riding shotgun in the front seat, when a loud Harley Davidson came towards them in the opposite lane. As it got closer they could clearly see the rider was in black leather and a bright yellow helmet with a reflective visor, just like Madame's. They all turned to watch it go by. Omigod! The rider had long grey hair! Oliver turned white.

- Jesus, Bucket! *Turn it around!*

A scream of tires as the big old car fishtails around and Bucket floors it and they take off after the Harley and its ghostly rider leading them back out of Malibu, with them yelling at Bucket to go faster after this apparition that looks just like Madame Joy, same outfit, same bike with the same chrome Springer front forks, and Oliver mumbling 'Oh, my god, oh, my god..." as the bike turns off the coast road and up into Topanga Canyon. They close in as the Canyon winds higher and finally - oh no! - it turns into Leo's hidden driveway and the guys all pile out of the car and run after the figure down into Leo's underground garage. Oliver is so scared he can barely keep up. The ghost rider dismounts and runs into a big store room, with the guys racing behind. Oliver nearly faints as he arrives in the room and takes in the scene.

The room is set up exactly like his office in the Red Cube. The figure is spread-eagle on the floor, face down, just like dead Madame Joy was, her grey hair splayed out. Oliver can hardly breathe, runs over to the dead figure and pulls her hair away and rolls her over. It's Leo.

They grab Oliver, shove him into a chair and slap him to stop him passing out from fright. They pump him with questions. Who was in the room? Who was it? Was it Macumba? *Was it Macumba?*

Holding his head like it's going to explode, he slides down onto the floor, rolling around, sobbing, arms wrapped tightly around his torso and yelling.

- Yes. Yes. *Yes! Yes! Yes!*

Sixty Three

Final Daze. That's how they billed the final concert. And the press release said that this time there would be one huge difference.

This time there would be no holograms. It would all be real.

A real stage, real props, real dancers, and the band would be out there onstage, finally able to hear the audience they were playing for. A treat.

Most important of all was that Omega Finn would be real, live, in person, on stage. No more tech magic. Just a performer and his fans.

There were no interviews, of course. He still had to be careful about showing his face in public, for his own safety. The few glimpses people had gotten of Oliver around the time of his arrest always showed him with his face covered. So Omega was still a mystery. He had to be. But in his blue paint and white wig, he would walk out onto that stage just like he used to at Rube's with Fear The Coming New York Earthquake. A mystery man still, but a real man.

The weeks leading up to the gig were the usual whirlwind of prep, rehearsals, and soundchecks, but this time there was also construction, real stages, real lighting, and they had decided to try to build one real giant Mickey Mouse hand, as big as the former holographic ones, but with pneumatics and hydraulics, so the fingers could actually move and the hand open and close and move around. It was a giant undertaking and a whole new world for Oliver and Leo to figure out, hiring an army of prop builders and experts in fields that were beyond their expertise. Leo said Oliver was nuts to try it. It could go wrong. It was dangerous.

They also decided to build a big red pyramid, to recall previous concerts, but this time a real one, not a hologram. For this reason it had to be not a smooth-sided pyramid but a ziggurat, a stepped pyramid, so that dancers could dance around it on every step from bottom to top, and appear and disappear through hinged walls on each side. Old school. Theatrical magic. Smoke and mirrors. No high tech. Madame Joy would have loved it, Oliver thought. Just like her old sideshows. But truly gigantic. Especially that monstrous mechanical hand

Sixty Four

Macumba was in Paris. She flew there with Fabien. There was an event there dearer to her heart than any other could ever be.

It was the anniversary of the funeral of Teetoo.

Ah, yes, dear reader, the sweet little bright green prince of all lizards had given up his small emerald ghost a little over a year after landing in Paris with Macumba, an illegal stow-away hiding in the hood of her warm woollen overcoat. He died peacefully in his sleep among the luxury cotton sheets of an exclusive Parisian hotel.

Macumba found him lying next to her on her pillow when she awoke, the yellow shafts of morning sunlight sparkling on the tiny scales of his fine aristocratic skin. She knew the moment she opened her eyes that he was dead and not just dreaming his dreams.

He had not been in the best of health since he left Brazil. It seems that Europe was simply too clean. Not enough bugs to hunt. Macumba had seen the gravity of the situation right away and had alerted a small army of exotic pet shop owners to the problem. But his new diet of French bugs simply was not up to the superior nutritional standards of their Brazilian brethren, and the loss of his greatest pleasure, the hunt, had seemed to sap his strength and the macho strut in his small stride.

Macumba could see what was slowly happening to her childhood friend and love of her life, but was powerless to stop it. Short of going back with him to the jungle, there was nothing she could do. Sending him back to Brazil to live with Olaf would have broken his little heart.

But his final year had been one of great celebrity and acclaim. From his dramatic introduction among Macumba's golden cornrows on the cover of *Vogue*, to his appearance at every gala, whether on her person like a living brooch that moved of its own accord, or asleep in her purse, Teetoo had become a superstar.

And among the immigrant *Banlieusards* of Paris, the poor millions of color, ignored by the rich in the stylish center, Teetoo was The Man! Not only was he the best buddy of their punk goddess, but was himself an illegal immigrant. That pushed his status over the top, from celebrity to a kind of worship. Teetoo was a meme.

In no time at all, Teetoo's image was everwhere, on graffiti walls from Paris to Istanbul, Harlem and the 'hoods of Los Angeles. In East LA, the Pachucos had his image painted on their bouncy low-rider Chevvies. And in Sao Paolo and Rio de Janeiro? Forget it. He was as big as Pele and not far behind the Virgin Mary.

If the funeral of Madame Joy in Hollywood was of a grandeur usually associated with movie stars and mafiosi, the death of little Teetoo in Paris turned into almost a state occasion.

There was no actual funeral. The French Roman Catholic church nixed the idea of using the sacred service for a lizard. But there was a colossal fuss online, padlocks were attached to bridges, there was a long parade behind the wee coffin made in the shape of a lizard and carried by Macumba surrounded by a massive security detail, and the burial in Paris's main pet cemetary was covered live everywhere in the world, attended by the Minister of Culture, and a few of the top fashion designers before Teetoo was entombed in a tiny mausoleum crowned by small sculpture of himself covered in gold leaf. To this day it gets more visits and flowers than those grander graves in the famous Pere LaChaise Cemetary nearby.

This anniversary of his funeral was marked on TV news from New York to Tokyo. And in Paris, the Teetoo Memorial Gala was like Mardi Gras. All the outer suburb immigrants dressed up in wild lizardy outfits and cavorted on flatbed trucks with bands and dancers, driving round and round the boulevards until the sweepers arrived and the sun came up.

It was glorious. Macumba was lavished with love and sympathy, but oh, how she missed her Teetoo. His absence made her feel so alone. Macumba was a superstar in Paris, and at the gala she was royalty. A year after the funeral the city's love for her felt even stronger, because she was so real. Success aside, she was still the jungle girl, the immigrant, the little colored girl with a punk autograph and her Yes, No, Maybe. She was as real as a child. It made her adorable. But vulnerable. And right now, she was helpless, the vessel of a deadly force. She was truly alone. Nobody could help her. And nobody but she even knew the whole terrible truth about her. Well, that's what she thought.

But Oliver and the boys knew now.

Sixty Five

Showtime! Giants Stadium was packed. The RedEyes were ready. The world was waiting. Every viewing device everywhere was beaming Final Daze. It seemed like every sentient being on the planet was glued to a screen. Holidays were declared everywhere, since employers knew that nobody would show up anyway. Essential workers in delivery rooms and nuclear submarines had one eye on their phones, beaming it.

Oliver and Leo had figured out the operation of their scary huge Mickey Mouse hand, and the many rehearsals of the dancers - a new experience for both guys - had gone well, with a few hitches, but the old Broadway motto that it would be 'alright on the night' held firm and, with crossed fingers, the lights went down, a colossal cheer went up in the big stadium and around the world, and the concert kicked off.

It was all real, all live. A real, old-fashioned rock concert with camera crews on gantries and tracks, swooping around the action, and drone cameras flying in and out, controlled by Leo and assistants, running through lists of cues and shots and sound guys tweaking volume on the fly, with the band bouncing around the stage like the days at Rube's, finally unleashed from their green screen, dodging cameras and bumping into each other and laughing at their own antics. Around the main red pyramid stage, dancers hoofed it along the different steps of the ziggurat and appeared and disappeared through the flaps and doors on cue while the pyramid pulsed and changed colors in sync with the music and a high-school band marched up and down the field in a jamboree of choregraphed fun and games. All live. All real. Wow.

Then came the much awaited appearance of the giant mechanical hand, rising up behind the red pyramid making a fist, a symbol of solidarity. The crowd in the stands pumped their fists and the viewers around the world maybe jumped up from their couches and pumped their fists too. And when the fist turned over and opened its fingers, revealing the little blue Omega just like when he had been a holograph, but real and right there, the stadium roar nearly drowned Bucket's power chords. There was a gasp as Oliver tripped and stumbled on the big white finger and rolled over onto the top step of the red pyramid. But he got up and bowed, laughing at his own clumsiness, just like a Broadway trooper. They loved it. He was *real!*

Macumba was backstage with the few invited guests, loving it all. She had flown in from Paris that morning and, having not seen rehearsals, so she was blown away like everyone else and feeling proud of Oliver for pulling it all off so brilliantly. More than that, she was relieved that he had decided to confront the fans and let them know that this was the end of The End, of Omega Finn and The Fear. She was not sure what he was going to say, but she loved him at that moment more than ever. She knew what a courageous thing it was he was about to do.

The gala had left her at peace with her loss of Teetoo. And on the flight back, she had reflected that all was finally turning out well for her and Oliver. His loss of Madame had broken his heart and the way she had died would always haunt him, and she felt crippled with remorse. But she would give him so much love in the life ahead of them that the joy she would bring would make up for the sorrow she had caused him.

But the terror she kept inside kept flashing through her mind. The rapist in the jungle. The near-killing in the junkyard. The dagger flying at Madame Joy. The gruesome deaths of the Gang of Four. All were her doing. None was intended. Would it stop? *Could* it stop?

A thunderous smack on the drums brought her thoughts back to the show. It was a triumph. Song after song, all his greatest hits, one after another, just like an old-school rock fest, blasted out around the stadium and around the world right up to the big finale when all the dancers emerged from the sides of the red ziggurat, all in blue paint and white wigs, dancing on every step right to the top step where Omega Finn himself danced alone, and at the last long power chord from the boys and the marching band down on the field, they all stood and held their hands up high, as did the crowd, and behind the red structure, the magnificent mechanical hand splayed it's fingers like a huge white fan spread behind Omega. Then above the hand, a huge Pentagraph appeared, glowing white, a nostalgic nod to former times, a hologram hanging in the air above the real hand, the real stage, the real dancers and the real Omega Finn. And the show was over. The crowd went nuts.

He tore off his white wig and waved it at the crowd, and stood there in his blue bodysuit, with his painted blue face grinning broadly at the cheering of the crowd. They loved him. It was a triumph. The stage was set for his 'little talk' to the millions. His farewell.

Sixty Six

Like the old-school theatrical affair that it set out to be, there were curtain calls, dancers ducking in and out of the flaps on the pyramid and the band taking bows. Oliver himself disappeared and then, after a break, came out alone to the roars of the crowd. The big white fingers were still splayed out behind him like a fan and the huge Pentagraph hologram shone above him. He was still wigless, all blue, with a blue face, as close to his real self as he dared be in public.

He stood there. The crowd slowly got quiet. He began to speak, quietly, frankly, all theatricality gone from his demeanor.

'Hello. My name is Oliver Finnegan. We have not met.' That is how he began, and there was complete silence as he continued. He told the story of Omega Finn exactly as it had happened, quite briefly, but from start to finish, from the bayous to the earthquake to the world cult that followed, not sparing himself any blame for the fear that he had instilled, merely saying that it had gained a momentum of its own, an inertia he could not control and apologized for any sadness that he had brought into the world. He was telling it as Oliver Finnegan, explaining that Omega Finn was just a stage name that had become a myth, a legend, credited with superhuman powers that he did not really have.

It was an honest explanation. An eloquent abdication.

But then his tone changed. He said he had a big surprise and that it would not be a pleasant one. He had a terrible duty to perform. He said that awful things had happened that he did not understand, the deaths of the Final Corp executives, and especially the murder of his beloved Madame Joy. He said his mind had always been a blank about that. But now he remembered. He remembered it in every detail.

Backstage, Macumba's eyes widened as she heard this. She slumped in her chair, her hand over her mouth, finding it hard to breathe.

Oliver continued. He said he had been accused of that killing, but someone else had been in that room with him. And the other person was the true murderer, not him. And that same person was also responsible for the other four savage killings that followed.

Backstage, unseen by the others, Macumba is quietly transforming. Her face is tortured, twisted, in terrible pain. She looks possessed.

Murmurs ripple through the crowd. They are clearly disturbed by this turn of events. Some mutter to each other, others try to shush them.

Oliver has to raise his voice and to speak more forcefully. He says that this murderer is in the audience tonight. There are loud gasps and a low hum of chatter at this shocking statement. He waits, dramatically, for the hubbub to calm down. It takes a while, but there is quiet again.

He begins to almost shout. He declares that in a few moments he will name this person. The crowd noise ramps up much louder and he now starts to really yell and to walk about the stage, jabbing the air with his hands to add emphasis. He says that he is standing here unprotected in order to give this person every chance to kill him right here and now, because if he does not say this person's name right now, he will be in danger for the rest of his life from this multiple murderer.

Backstage, Macumba, her face contorted, looks down at her hands. She makes the fingers of one hand slowly come together into a fist.

Behind Oliver, the massive hand begins to move. Its splayed fingers slowly start to come together into a fist. It starts to rise slowly above him. A few people in the crowd start to notice this and to nudge each other and point at the slowly forming giant fist that rises slowly above Oliver as he continues to challenge the murderer to kill him now so that he will not live in fear. He says he is now going to name the murderer.

He pauses. He waits. Behind him the huge fist rises directly above him, the crowd is pointing to it, fearful, as if to warn him.

He yells, "*It was Macumba! It was Macumba! It was Macumba!*"

Macumba raises her fist in the air and slams it down into the palm of her other hand. The gigantic fist crashes down on Oliver, crushing him underneath its colossal weight. The crowd all scream at the top of their lungs, eighty thousand voices screaming into the night, a high-pitched roar like an explosion, carrying across the river into the city, a noise like none other ever heard in New York.

Macumba, released from her trance by the deafening roar, runs to sees what she has done. The fist sits on top of the red pyramid and under it, her lover, or what is left of him, crushed to death. Blind with grief, she runs down the back stairs and onto the playing field. Cops stop her, but RedEyes recognize her and let her through. She finds her way up the inner stairs and arrives at the top of the pyramid as the fist slowly rises into the air again, and underneath it... there is nothing.

Sixty Seven

On a soundstage nearby, in front of a green-screen wall, surrounded by holography equipment, Oliver and Leo stare at a monitor. On it is a view of Macumba on her knees on the top level of the red pyramid, as the fist rises and moves back to its normal position behind it. There is nothing else there. No crushed body. Nothing. Just Macumba sitting there sobbing.

Oliver is dressed for green-screen action in a skin-tight outfit with the usual small white dots all over it to map his movements. Leo says,

- She fell for it! She killed a hologram. You know what you have to do.

- I can't do it. She's innocent. It's not my sweet Macumba who did that.

- Ollie! There's no difference! She *is* what she *does!* You have to do it! She'll kill you again! She's lethal! *She's out of control!*

On the top of the pyramid, looking broken and devastated, Macumba slowly stands up, racked with tears. Sobbing uncontrollably, she looks up at the shining Pentagraph towering above her and whispers, "Oh, Oliver, I'm so sorry. I'm so sorry."

Staring at the monitor, Oliver is just as lost in tears as Macumba. He reaches out to the screen to touch her image, tears pouring down.

- Quick Ollie. Do it now! She just killed you! She killed Madame! She killed them all! *She'll kill you again. She'll kill us all!*

- I can't do it!

- Then I can! It's the only way. Gimme that!

Leo grabs a remote from Oliver, as he buries his face in his hands.

- I'm doing it! OK, Ollie? I'm doing it now! *Yes? Yes?*

- Yes. OK. Do it. *Yes Yeeeeeesssssss!!!!*

Leo clicks a button on the remote. In the stadium, as Macumba stands there looking around at the crowd, lost in a daze, above her the blazing Pentagraph moves down towards her. The horizontal bars move closer together and drop right behind her as she stands there. It is now exactly as tall as she is. The Pentagraph moves towards her. *And it just keeps going.* It goes *right through her.* It slices her into five scorched, sizzling pieces that tumble down the ziggurat and lay on the ground by the red steps.

The crowd screams. RedEyes fall to their hands and knees, horrified at the sight of these seared, smoking sections of burnt human flesh that a moment ago were the sweet-natured, beautiful and beloved Macumba.

Sixty Eight

Everything in the show up to the last part had been real. Oliver had been whisked away in one of the choppers while the band and dancers were taking their bows, and flown to the green screen nearby, to be with Leo. So when he walked back out again, he was a hologram.

And nobody could tell the difference. Leo was that good.

Oliver had to shield himself from fatally dangerous Macumba, to be far away from whatever she might do after he invited her to kill him and she tried and failed. He knew he would have to kill her. It had to be done openly, immediately, right there and then, before she could try again.

Heartbreaking as it was, the killer voodoo had to be stopped. Macumba was no longer lovely, sweet Macumba. She was now just the murdering vessel she had become. People had to see that this evil had to die, that Macumba had to die in order to be saved and that *he had no choice.*

But she was so beloved that it was too much for anyone to take in, too sad for mere reason to prevail. When he put her out of her misery, he knew there would be riots in the stadium and everywhere in the world, especially in Paris and Brazil, until people finally came to accept that she really *was* the serial killer, the murderer who had killed Madame Joy and the others, and had even killed Omega Finn, right there in front of their eyes. So it had to be done this way. Openly. Publicly. Tragically.

But he also knew that until the world understood, he would be the most hated man on earth. He had, in just a few minutes, confessed to being a fraud, to having no supernatural powers, to making the world cough up billions of dollars in order to stay safe from a threat that didn't exist, via the biggest scam ever scammed. Then he had sliced into neatly cut pieces the most beloved woman on earth, who now lay in those same lumps of smoking flesh on the ground in front of all the horrified people he had just confessed to.

He had killed her to save her. Time would make that clear, surely. Wouldn't it? Time would absolve him, surely. Wouldn't it?

He thought that eventually everyone would see he *had* to do what he did, that there was no other way, and that they would forgive him.

He was wrong. They never forgave him.

Sixty Nine

It was time to disappear. And he did. Completely. Oh, his music stayed around, that slinky, sexy, grown-up rock 'n' roll. But slowly it faded from DJ lists and eventually the very name Omega Finn was so toxic that, well, you just don't hear it any more. And the CDs that once were such powerful amulets? Shoveled into landfill out of pure collective embarrassment at having been so totally fooled.

There were the usual conspiracy rogues, of course, who kept up the fiction that the real Omega Finn truly was a magical being and was being held by the Deep State in some secure desert location for... oh, for whatever bullshit they came up with. Those people will believe anything. And there will always be Pentagraph tattoos on kids who just want to act tough. But apart from that... that train is long gone.

But Macumba, ah, lovely Macumba, magical Macumba. Her funeral made those of Madame Joy and Teetoo seem modest by comparison, because there were so many of them all over the world. The overtones of black magic surrounding her death, meant that no church could ever condone an official event. But that just made her adoring fans create their own funerals, everywhere. It just felt like the whole world was in mourning.

She was not only forgiven, she was placed on a cloud of stardust in her own private paradise, to be paid hommage to, worshiped and revered by everyone from hopeless teenage romantics, to those of us who simply appreciate the ironies of life, because, yes, she was guilty, but...

Guilty but blameless. Guilty but helpless. Guilty but innocent.

Guilty but the most sweet-natured, loveable, kind, generous and stunningly beautiful girl the world has ever seen, a role model of simple goodness to every child on the planet.

She was also quite possibly the most tragic person who ever lived.

This little book, dear reader, is dedicated to her memory, and to the memory of her little Teetoo, prince of lizards, patron saint of all illegal immigrants, and gentleman.

Together they brought love, beauty and joy into the world.

The End

The end of The End is the final surprise.

The most notorious and most pursued man on Earth is not in an armed compound on a private island, nor locked away on some heavily fortified superyacht on the high seas. The shocking truth is that he lives among us, unnoticed. And single.

In New York, Paris, Tokyo, Rio and in other cities, under other names, he owns a quite modest apartment or beach house, but nothing too showy or fancy. No superyacht. No plane. Nothing to bring any attention to the multi-zillionaire wealth that he still has.

Any way that his identity could be discovered has been erased. For every home he bought, he used different lawyers. Escorts don't know they just spent the night with such a notorious man. Folks meet him all the time and don't recognize him. It's surprising how little is needed to change a man. A nose job, a new hair color, tinted contact lenses, and there you are. Not there.

I met him myself and only later did he tell me that it was he I had been talking to over a beer in Bangkok. Years before that, I had interviewed him for a music magazine and spent hours with him at that time, and I still didn't guess that this rather sad-looking man in the bar talking baseball, was him. Since that evening, I have spent hours on the phone with him for this book, always sensing that same quiet sadness, always wondering what he looks like this time.

His band is gone, but it's hard to imagine they're not still close, since they were all kids together. Maybe they're in Mexico, or even back in the bayous, shielded from strangers. As for Leo, good luck in tracking down that whisp of human fog.

The Fear Building was sold and is again the Flatiron Building. The Red Cube has been 're-purposed' and is unrecognizable. The Gang Of Four are all dead. Madame Joy is dead. Teetoo is dead. Macumba is dead. The whole astonishing, scary global cult of Omega Finn is dead.

And Oliver? Is he, at least, still alive and well?

No. He is alive.

New York. Hollywood. Bangkok.

www.theendtheendtheend.com

Made in the USA
Monee, IL
29 September 2022

14728043R00080